CHEESE LORDS

CHEESE RUNNERS TRILOGY
BOOK THREE

BY
CHRIS A. JACKSON

ISBN 1939837146
ISBN-13 978-1939837141

Cover art by Brian King

Acknowledgements

Thanks so much to Bryan King for the cover art and to Charles Crawford for the cover concept. Special thanks to Jeff Breslauer for the idea to produce the story as an audiobook, and for bringing my characters to life with his great voice work.

CHAPTER ONE

THE BIG CHEESE

Record # KR29387/γ. Transcript begins:

Corinthian leather creaked faintly as I settled into my new chair.

It was a nice chair. Remind me to thank a Corinthian cow next time we get one. I fiddled with the remote, adjusting the arm rests, the back, and the height until it matched my most relaxed posture perfectly.

Perfectly…

Why is it you never hear of Corinthian steak or Corinthian milk? Or Corinthian cheese, for that matter? Hmm…remind me to look into this whole Corinthian thing.

Yes, sometimes it's nice being the Big Cheese. I won't tell you there aren't any perks with the position of CEO of Wisconsin Cheese. You'd never believe me. I mean, we rake in more real income than every other business, legal or illegal, on the planet, so we've got a lot of discretionary funds to dispose of.

Perks…yeah, I *like* perks.

I lifted my self-warming coffee cup and sipped my freshly brewed coffee, lightened to just the right color with *real* cream. There's something almost euphoric about that first sip of perfect coffee. The president of the United Earth Government doesn't lighten *her* coffee with *real* cream. She has to use that gloppy synthetic stuff.

I sipped and sighed…ah, yes. It's good to be the Big Cheese.

A buzzer went off on my desk.

If you ran over a small marsupial with a steam roller, it would probably mimic the tone of my desk buzzer nicely.

I *hate* my desk buzzer.

I brushed the boiling hot coffee from my Ever-Klean® jumper—so much for truth in advertising—and checked my watch: 7:58.

Okay, *most* of the time it's good to be the Big Cheese.

I punched the button and said, "It's only seven-fifty-eight. I'm not in yet."

"You sound in," said the voice from the outer office. We'll get to that in a second.

"I'm not. I'll be in at eight. Not before."

"If you're not in, who made the coffee?"

"Gremlins made the coffee."

"Good coffee for gremlins."

"Thanks."

"Oh, so you *did* make the coffee."

"Uh, yeah." Damn. The voice was Gertrude, my secretar…uh…administrative assistant.

Gertrude is probably the best administrative assistant on Earth. She's certainly the most expensive. We can afford the best, and we get it. The problem is she's also one of the less-than-perky perks of being the Big Cheese.

I think Gertrude is actually the devil. Or maybe the devil's administrative assistant. Yeah, that sounds about right.

"I'm adjusting my new chair and enjoying a well-earned cup of coffee, Gertrude. A cup of coffee I had to make myself, which ate considerably into the time I would get to enjoy it."

"I *know* you're not suggesting that *I* should make your coffee."

"Other administrative assistants make coffee, Gertrude."

"Other administrative assistants aren't *me*, sir."

"A fact for which I thank the laws of genetics. I'm not in until eight." My tact has not improved with my promotion to CEO, just in case you wondered.

"Yes, *sir*."

The intercom went dead. I sipped my coffee and tried to relax, but it was useless. I knew the Buzzer from Hell would go off in fifty-four seconds.

I didn't ask to be the Big Cheese, and even though I've probably got one of the best chairs in the solar system, I'm not all that happy with being stuck in it. I'd much rather be captain of the *Limburger*. Granted, someone else has to deal with Turk and Mishi—that's the good part—but that same someone else also gets to fly around the cosmos watching Kik get in and out of the pilot's couch—that's the not-so-good part. Some part of me also misses the danger, adventure, and intrigue of running the most illegal controlled substance in the galaxy right under the noses of our Farfnian overlords.

Okay, so maybe I'm a little quirky.

Then there's the paperwork. Invoices and manifests, and payroll, and vacation, and paternity leave—damn Zook anyway. And there are the *real* headaches: the French, our fiercest competitors; the Farfnians, an ever-present threat; the Sploig, an invisible and even greater threat; and my secretary—oops, sorry, *administrative assistant*—an all-too-visible-and-every-bit-as-menacing-as-a-Sploig-robosassin-which-aren't-so-bad-once-they've-been-reprogrammed threat.

Then there are the meetings: meetings with captains, meetings with sanitation, meetings with production, meetings with management, meetings with security, meetings with the milkers' union, meetings with the president of the (expletive deleted) HUBCAP nutcases, who seem to think they're doing *us* a favor by violently opposing the extermination of every cow on the planet.

Frankly, I'd rather negotiate with a squad of Farfnian marines.

On the upside, I have made some improvements to how Wisconsin Cheese does business. First of all, the whole fleet's running in and out of WCC without ever flying into or out of The Barn. We transformed one pasture into a landing pad so they could use patches of grass as homing beacons for the stringspace shift. Stringless stringspace jumping is now standard practice, and is even being automated on some ships. As a result, every WCC ship is quickly becoming a miniature zoo, with creatures from half the planets in the spiral arm kept in tidy little cages. Which means that PETA's on my ass now, too.

And if those weren't enough…

The door to my office burst open without so much as a knock or even a buzz from Gertrude. This should have been impossible, since there is a robosassin stationed just outside programmed to keep anyone from entering unannounced or unwanted. But since the person entering also did the programming, I wasn't particularly surprised.

"Harry! Look!" Zook's jumper was open to the waist and he was pointing to a big, red lump on his chest. It was about the size of a baseball and it looked inflamed.

"You really ought to have a doctor look at that, Zook. Looks like some kind of infection."

"This is my *son*, Harry!"

"Your son?"

"Or my daughter, or…well, neither really. Actually, we don't have sexes, but—"

"You mean Sparky wasn't a girl?"

"Uh, no. All Immortals are the same sex. We exchange genetic material when we shake hands. Anyway, he's pregnant now, too."

"Oh, great. Well, that's *his* problem, or its problem, I guess. Sorry, Zook, but I always thought of you as male. I can't get my head around you being pregnant."

"Neither can I, Harry." He poked the reddened lump and winced. "This is completely new for me! Isn't it interesting? Look, I think I'm getting another one here!" He pointed to his stomach just below his ribcage where there was a slight swelling.

"Twins?"

"Who knows?" he said, far too cheerful for one who was budding like a prize rose bush. "Could be more, or it could just be one big one trying to get out in more than one place."

"Trying to get out?"

"Well, yes. It, or they, have to get out somehow."

"What will it look like? Your…uh…offspring I mean."

"I have no idea!" Again, *way* too cheerful and downright freaky.

"You don't know what your own children will look like? Don't tell me you've never seen one."

"Well, we don't reproduce very often, and I don't have very clear memories of my own childhood, Harry. Ooo! Is that coffee? Do you mind?"

Before I could protest, he grabbed my perfect cup of coffee and downed it in one swallow.

"Sorry. I'm having cravings."

Great. A pregnant Immortal with cravings. What next?

"Uh, no problem. There's more if you want it."

"No thanks. You wouldn't have any vinegar, would you?"

"No. Sorry, Zook, I'm fresh out of vinegar. So what does a shapeshifter do to…uh…prepare to have babies?"

"I don't have a clue. Oh, we're not really shapeshifters. Not like the Sploig. We're just mimics. I could mimic you if I wanted to, but that would just be confusing."

"Yeah, I think one Harry Fische is enough. But your kids will be mimics, too, so I guess they'll need someone or something to mimic. Right?"

"I hadn't thought of that." He sounded positively gleeful. "Maybe I should start looking for volunteers."

"Hey, that's right. You get to pick what your kids look like! That's so cool!"

"Isn't it wonderful?" Zook was obviously enjoying his pregnancy more than anything he'd done in the last few centuries, and I didn't want to depress him, so I played along.

"Yeah. Wonderful," I said, wondering if the little beastie or beasties would be dangerous before they found someone to mimic. "Should we take any precautions for the…um…event? I mean, I don't want anyone to get hurt, or mimicked by accident."

"Oh. I hadn't thought of that." His eyes got a little wide. "I suppose putting me in isolation might be a good idea, but it won't be for a while yet, I think." He poked the bump on his chest and winced. "Maybe."

"Does it hurt?"

"Oh, yes! Excruciatingly!" He grinned as if the pain was something he was proud of. He fished a small bottle from a pocket of his jumper and took a swallow.

"Does that help?" I asked, thinking it must be some kind of pain killer.

"Not really, but it blunts the cravings."

"What is it?" I really should know better.

"Furniture polish."

Did I mention just how truly alien Zook can be sometimes? Well, this was one of those times. The hairs were standing up in little rows on the back of my neck. I don't know if he is really that strange or if he just gets jazzed up by freaking me out. If I ever find out it's the latter, I'll strangle him.

"Tell you what, Zook, I'll call down to the cafeteria and have the chef make you whatever you want, okay?"

"Thanks, Harry, but could you call the chief mechanic as well? I've been dying for French vanilla ice cream topped with forty-weight motor oil all morning."

"Whatever you want, Zook. Just don't poison yourself." Yep, freaking me out on purpose, I'm sure of it.

"How did *you* get in here?" Gertrude called from the door, a datapad in one hand and a pot of coffee in the other.

"I walked." Zook really should learn when to shut up. "Ooo, is that more coffee?" He advanced on Gertrude fearlessly, which just shows you how alien he really is. The aforementioned squad of Farfnian marines would be afraid of Gertrude, and rightfully so.

Gertrude is a…uh…formidable woman, and not just because she tips the scales at about a hundred forty kilos. I know I told you that the Farfnians gave us a cure for fat, but some people like to be…um…big, and since we have cures for all the bad things that go along with being gravity challenged, some opt to stay supersized. But, like I said, though her bulk is daunting, Gertrude's true power lies in her job. She is, arguably, the most powerful secretary in the solar system. She wields more real power than any head of state you can name and could crush the entire Earth military-industrial complex with a single phone call. She faxes CEOs into oblivion, could file your entire life away so that your mother couldn't find it, and shakes alien governments with her emails.

She is…Super-Secretary! Oh, I know, but Super-Administrative Assistant sounds stupid.

"Yes, you Immortal weirdo, it's coffee, and it is *not* for you!"

"Harry said I could have some," he said, reaching for the pot.

"Well, I'm not Harry! Now keep your grabby little Immortal paws off my pot!" She pulled it out of his way and blocked him with the datapad.

"Zook, please. I'll get you more coffee. I'm calling for your forty-weight sundae right now."

He froze and looked at me. "With espresso bean sprinkles?"

"Sure. Whatever you want." I tried not to imagine what the combination of sugar, caffeine and motor oil would do to an alien metabolism. I'd be lucky if he didn't spontaneously combust.

"Mmmm, sounds delicious." He turned to go. "Thanks, Harry!"

"He's even weirder than usual today," Gertrude said, moving her bulk to my desk and filling my cup. She produced a little packet of cream from somewhere on her person where my imagination simply refused to go and lightened my coffee.

Okay, so maybe she's not the devil's administrative assistant.

Isn't it strange how coffee makes everyone less devilish? I just hope the Farfnians never find out just how addicted humans are to it. They might hold Earth's coffee supply ransom for information on the cheese producers. Now, I wouldn't sell the WCC down the river for a cup of java, but after a month without coffee, the entire Earth would probably be nothing but a wasteland of wandering zombie-faced maniacs, ripping each other to pieces with no provocation.

Imagine Monday morning…forever.

Yep, they'd sell us out quicker than a lawyer can insert a contingency clause.

"Thank you, Gertrude." I sipped…perfect. "So, what's on the agenda today?"

"Six meetings, three conference calls, and a pile of paperwork three feet high on my desk." She passed me the datapad and I flipped through the itinerary. "Oh, and lunch with the Carpoolian ambassador. I took the liberty of ordering takeout."

"After the lunch, I hope."

"Do I *look* like I want to take your dry cleaning out after you barf all over your suit? The lunch is at noon in Minneapolis, so I booked you a driver. We can work on some of the paperwork on the road."

"Wonderful." Somehow sharing a backseat with Gertrude sounded only slightly less appetizing than lunch with a Carpoolian. "Anything specific on the agenda for lunch, or just the usual?"

"The usual. I packed a briefcase for you. Two million farfs in bearer bonds."

"That's the usual?"

"Well, the price of a good bribe has gone up since the Carpoolians discovered politics, Harry."

"Fine. What about the conference calls?"

"Two unions, and one with Jean-Verne Routois."

"Uh-oh." Jean-Verne Routois is the president of Bongrain, Besnier, and Bel, or BBB, the biggest cheese producer in France. "What does he want?"

"What do the French always want? They want the whole world to be French." I knew she was joking, but I refused to bite. She scowled at me and said, "Your recent success is cutting in on the whole cheese market, Harry. Prices are dropping, interdiction efforts are up, and the Carpoolians are learning government. Everyone blames you; what do you think he wants?"

"Uh, I don't know. My fondue recipe?"

She didn't laugh at my joke either, so I guess that made us even. I noticed that the call with Jean-Verne was first on the agenda. Well, no sense putting off the inevitable. I was hoping I could have delayed this little confrontation, but with WCC tripling its production and undercutting every other cheese producer on the planet for the last three months, a call like this had to come eventually.

"First things first, Gertrude. Buzz me when J-V's on the phone."

"Just don't call him 'J-V' again, Harry. The last time you did that, I got a two-hour lesson in etiquette from his assistant."

"So, did you learn anything?"

"Yes. Don't call Jean-Verne 'J-V'. You really should learn not to piss everyone off so much, Harry. You'll live longer."

"Well, I have it on good authority that immortality is highly overrated, but thanks." She left the office to give me some time to prepare. Then it hit me—no, not the coffee, but now that you mention it, I did take a quick break to the little CEO's room before the conference call. Why would this be a conference call if Jean-Verne was the only one calling?

There could be only one answer: they were calling in the Big Cheeses from all over Earth to gang up against me.

Oh, wonderful…

CHAPTER TWO

SWEET SUCCESS

The problem with illicit gain, it turns out, is what to do with it. WCC has about a dozen phony corporations it uses to launder money. Remember that emu burger you had for lunch? Well, part of that eight hundred dollars went back to me, heh heh… The trick with these little scams is to keep the currency in farfs, not dollars. I mean, why learn alchemy if all you can do is change gold into lead?

Laundering is actually the easy part; what to do with the money once it's clean, now *that* was the real difficulty.

I never really thought I'd have to ask myself how to dispose of twenty billion farfs, but, aside from upgrading our ships, breeding more cows, extending our underground facilities, buying some really killer office furniture, and setting up a standing order for some of the best scotch on the planet, I'd kinda ran out of stuff to want. Then I got the phone call.

So, how do you handle it when your fiercest competitor calls you up and says, "You can't keep doing this!"

Well, more precisely, he said, "Ju caan't keep doing zis, 'arry!" even before the static of the encrypted connection cleared enough for me to see Jean-Verne's bulbous eyes focused upon mine.

Wow, not even an "Ello." He was pissed.

"And good morning to you," I said, remembering Gertrude's emphasis on etiquette. "And what exactly am I doing, Jean-Verne?" I asked innocently as six other faces coalesced in the split multi-screen. The Biggest Cheeses in the world all scowled at me like I'd just revoked their library cards. Of course, I knew exactly what he was suggesting that I could no longer do; I'm not that stupid.

No, *really*!

"Jhu are ruining aur business, 'arry! Our contracts wis ze Carpoolians 'ave been wrapped up in political red tape, and ze price of cheese az gone down ze toilet'." His pencil-thin moustache twitched when he spoke, and the corners of his mouth were turned down in a most comical manner.

Yep, pissed all right. And the rest of them looked no happier.

You know, until becoming CEO, the thought never really crossed my mind that I should regret putting the pinch on other cheese producers. I mean, isn't that kinda the point of business, to outdo your competitors?

Trouble was, I *did* feel bad about it. I guess I'm not such a devout capitalist after all.

I had done a little discreet searching on the nets, and the economies of the UK, France, Canada, Italy, Germany, Australia, Spain, and the few other cheese-producing areas—not nations any more, but we still put on pretenses—were doing rather poorly. The money we cheese runners pump into our local economies gets distributed around and improves things, which, aside from getting rich, was the point of doing all this in the first place. Granted, we're crooks, smugglers, cheese runners, and corrupters of the Farfnian upper-middle class, but our real goal here was to pump money into the Earth economy. But with money comes power, and with power comes control, and with control comes responsibility, and with responsibility comes the overwhelming recognition of the fact that every decision you make could mean life or death for millions of human beings.

Remind me why we were doing this again?

Oh, yeah, money.

Not being masters of our own destiny in the galactic community or anything like that…right?

Yeah, I *thought* it was the money. Maybe I am a capitalist after all.

Well, things were getting a little lopsided. Our success, brief but profound, had pumped about ten times the usual amount of capital into our economy. The good old U S of A was starting to stick out like a cockroach on a china plate. The easy solution—well, it sounded easy—was to bring everyone else up to speed on our newly discovered delivery techniques. But just try to set up a meeting between more than a hundred different companies in one place when they don't—or won't—speak the same language and have been competing against one another for decades.

I didn't even try.

No, instead I took the "Harry Approach." Yes, that means I pissed everyone off to the point where they could no longer ignore me. Then I miraculously got this phone call. The competition was now coming to me, and I was holding all the cards. For perhaps the first time in my sordid life, I felt the rush of negotiating from a position of power.

Yeah, power…that's almost as good a perk as a cushy chair.

Tell me I'm not a genius.

"I'm sorry your dealings with the Carpoolians have been disrupted, Jean-Verne, but what makes you think I had anything to do with it?" Okay, I knew he wasn't so dim as to not know what we all knew, but I also knew he didn't know *how* what was happening was happening. You know?

Why are you looking at me like that?

What do you mean, confusing? All I said was he knew we were undercutting his business, but not how.

I *did* say that the first time!

Oh, never mind. Here, I'll buy the next round. A scotch for me, and a Turpenoid tonsillectomy for my friend here.

(sound of ice and liquid filling several glasses, and a muffled explosion)

There, feel better? I don't know how you drink that stuff.

Anyway, Jean-Verne wasn't buying it for a second, and neither, it seemed, were the others. Lord Brenton Colston of Earlswood, England's most secretive and select producer of designer cheeses, scowled so hard he could have curdled milk into whey.

"Now see here, *Mister* Fische. We know you have some means of distributing product without the Farfnians getting wind of it. You're driving down the price of cheese throughout the quadrant. You're ruining us, and you don't give a damn!"

"Not exactly true, Lord Colston," I countered, wondering just how one gets a title in the post-Farfnian world. Did Queen Diana give out knighthoods for running cheese?

"Yer bonkers, mate! Wa've been wochin' yer operation fo wakes!" Lonny MacAllen of Roo-Cheese, Inc. rapped his knuckles on the monitor, making his face wobble like a wallaby on cocaine. "No' a sangle ship 'as left yo' baaan, and the maaket's flaaded with Wisconsin's prodaact. Wha'a ya up to, bloke?"

"That *is* true," I said, sipping my perfect coffee and leaning back in my perfect chair. "I admit that we've modified our shipping and distribution operation. What *wasn't* true was that I don't care."

"What?" Colston's cheeks bulged until I thought his face might explode.

"I said that I *do* care, and I'm willing to not only share the technology that has enabled us to upgrade our transportation and distribution systems, but also let you all in on exactly how we came to be in possession of that technology."

They all stared at me like I'd just turned blue. I looked down at my hands just in case, but they were still the same old pinkish-tan. Whew, that had me worried for a moment.

"Jhu are jhoking," Jean-Verne said accusatively, as only the French can be accusative.

He obviously wanted me to rise to the bait and divulge the proof of my ridiculous claim right then and there, but Harry Fische was not, in fact, born yesterday, although Zook might disagree with me on that point. When you consider Zook's lifespan, I wasn't born yesterday, I was born about forty-five minutes ago. Maybe that's why he seems so alien; the rest of us are just a passing *thing* to him, like the omelet I had for breakfast. He'll turn around one day and I'll be dead of old age, and he'll just pick out another younger, healthier human or alien to hang around and go on about his business.

Yeah, that's what freaks me out about Zook.

"No, Jean-Verne, I am unfortunately *not* joking. There's more at stake here than the cheese market. We've got enemies, and I don't mean the Farfnians. These enemies want Earth's cheese. And not *just* the cheese, but the ability to make their *own* cheese."

Exclamations of astonishment, disbelief, and gastrointestinal distress—gotta love the Italians—filled my split-screen. Finally, Jean-Verne raised a hand and silenced the others, proving beyond a doubt that they had worked this all out among themselves beforehand. He was their spokesman, their Ambassador-des-Cheese, so to speak.

"Jhu are insane! Vat proof do jhu 'ave of zis ludicrous claim?"

I could have expounded upon his lack of etiquette, but I decided to quash—Yes, *quash.* I was definitely in a quashing mood—his rebuttal with one simple word.

"Tillamook."

Okay, maybe it's not such a simple word.

That put a damper on their ire, at least for the moment. All seven of them looked as if they'd just finished lunch and discovered that the chef was Carpoolian. The discomfort on their faces was almost worth the billions of farfs I was going to lose on this deal.

"Vat do jhu know of Tillamook?"

"My dear Jean-Verne, I know *everything* about what happened to Tillamook, who did it, and why." I'd bribed enough Farfnian cruiser captains to know when I had my opponent beat, and these poor saps were done. Like poke-'em-with-a-fork done. Just to prove I'm a nice guy, I thought I'd throw them a tidbit. "That is why I intend to share what we've discovered. It's not just about cheese anymore, ladies and gentlemen, it's about Earth."

I'd been thinking about this since the first day I sat down in this office. I knew we'd have to share our findings with the other cheese producers, but I didn't think it would happen so soon. If I held out much longer, I'd risk dissension in our own ranks; we might be competitors, but we were still on the same side. No cheese producer had ever ratted out another, but with every other dairy on the planet at a disadvantage because of our new practices, there could be only one end to the dispute. And since I've always worked very hard to avoid becoming a tiny bit of burnt meat at the bottom of a meteorite impact crater, I had known that I would share the secret of stringless stringspace travel and the Sploig technology with every other cheese runner on the planet since the moment we discovered it.

Not only that, but this was really the only way we would ever beat the Farfnians, not to mention the Sploig. Earth had to unite or we were doomed to forever be nothing but a backward little third-class planet on the ass end of the universe.

Wow, how philosophical can you get?

It must be the chair. Yeah…that's it…the chair.

"So, whadaya gonna do then, ay Fische? This new technology thing you got; you gonna share it with us, then?" Carol Brunte, the Canadian Consolidated Cheese Consortium representative, had her usual cut-through-the-crap attitude turned on full.

"Yes, I am, but not right now, and not only with you. That would be as unfair as keeping it for myself." That drew quite a few more raised eyebrows.

"Oh, so yer givin' it ta everybody, then?"

"Well, I think I might leave the Farfnians out of the loop, but yes, I plan to invite every cheese producer on Earth to a meeting, and there I'll tell everyone what we've found and how we found it."

They all stared at me some more until Lord Colston broke the silence.

"And where exactly will we be having this Cheesemoot?"

"Cheesemoot; I like that. I'll get Gertrude started on the invitations. I think neutral ground would be best for our little moot. Apollo Station okay with everyone?"

"Ze Palace, I presume?" Jean-Verne asked, making a face that French waiters everywhere have perfected.

"The Palace de Luna it is." It was either that or the lobby of the Motel Eight, since those were the only two places to stay on the Moon. Apollo Station is a huge city, but it's more of an industrial complex than a tourist Mecca. They don't have much in the way of amenities except for The Palace, and that was built to the hilt for entertaining corporate bigwigs.

"Shall we say…" I tapped my calendar, relishing which meeting I would obliterate with the click of a button. Ah, yes, the Bovine Groomer's Association meeting…perfect. "Four o'clock PM, GMT next Thursday?"

"Zat will be fine," Jean Verne said without even a glance to his cohorts. Not one of them argued.

A chill trickled down my spine that my chair should not have allowed. I wondered if he actually had the power to answer for the group, or if I was talking to a Sploig. If the Sploig had infiltrated Earth's cheese-production facilities, we were in trouble.

"WCC will pick up the tab." It was the least I could do. Well, not really; nothing would have been the least I could have done, but I was feeling magnanimous. Yeah, that's me, Mr. Magnanimous. "I'm thinking a nice formal dinner, for openers. I'll give everyone the basics there, and we'll get to the technical details on Friday. We will, of course, require a simple security check for everyone who attends."

"Of course, Monsieur Fische, as we will of you and yours.

"Very well. My assistant will contact you with the details."

I cut the connection and called Gertrude. I told her about the trip, and she told me to make my own damned vacation plans. I explained who I was meeting there, and she reluctantly agreed to set things up. She had a lot of calls to make. Wisconsin Cheese is one of the biggest producers on the planet, but there are a lot of other fish in the sea.

Or there used to be, until the Farfnians decided they liked seafood. It's a shame about all the whales. Oh, sorry. I got sidetracked.

I really didn't have that tight a calendar; I could have scheduled the meeting for the next day, in fact, but there were a lot of arrangements to be made, and there was one really good reason to put it off a few days. If I was flying to the moon, there was only one way I wanted to get there, and I knew exactly who I wanted to do the driving.

I put in a call for the new captain of the *Limburger* to change his schedule when he got back from his current trip. He'd be taking a little side run to Apollo Station.

CHAPTER THREE

TAKE ME TO THE MOON

Okay, I was calling a meeting of every single CEO of every single cheese producer on Earth. There are one hundred forty-three of us, in case you wondered; most are simple little mom-and-pop operations with only one or two ships, but I had asked everyone. And with everyone in one place, security was high on my priority list.

I let Gertrude handle it.

I focused on more personal issues, like what to wear, my speech, what Kik should wear—be still my fibrillating heart—and who to have as my personal bodyguard. I was vacillating between Turk and a robosassin, and yes, I do mean vacillating. I decided on both. Paranoid? Me? (expletive deleted) right I'm paranoid.

But what really scared the crap out of me was that I saw no way around bringing Zook along. Nobody else could handle the Sploig technology, and we might just need a few magic tricks if things didn't turn out right.

But Zook wasn't looking so good. I'd decided to visit him in his quarters, the only place I *could* visit him, since I'd isolated him for everyone's safety and well-being.

"I really don't know if it is a good idea, Harry," he said, polishing off the last of a headcheese and beer float. I tried very hard not to barf. The headcheese had been a gift from Jean-Verne; it was either bury it or give it to Zook, so I asked him if he wanted it. Big mistake.

But I had dined with Carpoolians, so this was really only mildly nauseating.

Uh-huh…

"Come on, Zook. It'll be fun." I tried to ignore him as he waddled over to his little fridge and opened the door. He'd gained a little weight in the past few days. In fact, he'd gained a *lot* of weight, and never stopped eating. He currently tipped the scales at about one hundred kilos, and had broken out in fist-sized bumps all over his now-bulbous body. He could barely navigate his quarters without tripping simply because he couldn't see his feet.

It didn't help that the floor was strewn with a million different gadgets, none of which I could identify, even accessing my Glactopedia program. I think most of it was Sploig bits and bobs from the vehicle we'd captured. We'd hired some of the best technical minds in the world, but no one except Zook had made much progress. Okay, I admit that we hadn't actually *captured* the vehicle as much as crashed on top of it and inadvertently taken it with us when we departed what could have otherwise turned into a sticky situation, but the result was the same.

"Fun?" he asked in a tone that told me that he wouldn't miss this trip for all the headcheese in France. He just wanted to be talked into it.

Frankly, the fact that I was starting to understand Zook scared me spitless, and it's hard to pronounce your s's when you're spitless, so what I said next came out sounding like, "Of courth it'll be fun! With the Thploig and the Farfnianth both watching uth like hawkth, what are the chantheth of everything going thmoothly?"

"You really think something might go wrong?" he asked, raising an eyebrow and smiling that quirky Immortal grin I had grown to know and dread. He stuck his head in the fridge and came out with something that looked suspiciously like a chicken liver and papaya sandwich on rye bread.

I checked my gag reflex and shrugged.

"Uh, well, not really. Not with Gertrude handling security, but we might get lucky." Okay, he had to know I was saying whatever I could think of to try to get him to come along, but maybe he wasn't thinking clearly. Pregnancy can do weird enough things to *humans*; what it had done to Zook's alien metabolism I couldn't even guess.

"You know, I am feeling rather strange about this, Harry."

Well, that was a no-brainer. Zook is *always* strange.

"How so?" I had to ask.

"While I am intrigued by the possibility of being caught between the Farfnians and the Sploig, which would truly test my capacity to manage crisis situations, I am reluctant to risk the lives of my unborn offspring."

"Oh, I hadn't thought of that." I really hadn't, which made me feel like a heel. "Forget it, Zook. Stay here and have your…uh…I mean…"

"I understand, Harry, but I also want very badly to go with you." He took a bite of his sandwich and spoke as he chewed. "I would not be pregnant at all if you had not given me the opportunity to meet another Immortal."

He swallowed, and I managed not to regurgitate my breakfast. "Uh, I guess I understand." Actually, I didn't understand at all.

"Good. Then I will go, but I must insist that I stay on the *Limburger*."

"Oh, of course. I mean, that's where you'll do the most good anyway. If things get dicey, you can just teleport us out like you did the robosassin, right?"

"Well, I don't know. I might be able to, but it requires a lot of power. Maybe not all of you at once."

"Good enough." Good enough as long as my name was at the top of the list of teleportees. "As soon as the *Limburger* lands, start getting your gear aboard."

"Okay, Harry," he said, grinning that mischievous Immortal grin of his. "You are going to enjoy telling the new captain he is giving us a ride, aren't you?"

"More than you can guess, Zook," I admitted, allowing myself a mischievous grin of my own.

***

"This is a stringship, not a ferry boat!" The former CEO of the WCC glared at me through the view screen, his face the color of a prize petunia.

"This is a WCC stringship, Ernie. And it goes where I say it goes, with or without its current captain." I enjoyed addressing my former boss by his first name almost as much as I enjoyed the hue of his deflating hubris. Okay, weak pun, but I couldn't resist. Turk turned from his console and grinned, which added even more to the degree of perk I was achieving with this call. The *Limburger* had just landed, and I had taken it upon myself to break the news to the ship's short-tempered captain.

I had felt a little guilty about unleashing him upon my old crew, but I couldn't very well just cut my old boss loose on the world. Not with what he knew. And having him killed would have been…uh…well… Bear with me, I'm trying to find a downside here.

Immoral? Nah…

Unethical? Nope…

Sinful? Not religious…

Too expensive to hide the body?

Hey, yeah. That's a *good* reason!

So I gave him the *Limburger* to console his hurt feelings, and told my crew to please not shove him out an airlock at the first opportunity…or the second opportunity. Oh, and I gave them all raises. *Good* crew.

"And who will pay for this little trip to the Moon, Fische? Three days will cost us half a trip. That's about fifty million farfs. Who's going to compensate us for that?"

"I will, Ernie. I'll pay the whole crew exactly half of what they just earned on your last run. How's that?"

"Uh…including bonuses?"

"Yes, including bonuses."

"Well…" He obviously wasn't used to getting what he asked for the first time he asked for it, which made it worth every farf. "That's fine. But you don't need the whole crew for this."

"No, I don't. You can give the cargo handlers and half the security team the days off at half pay. Keep the animal handlers on board. It'd take more time to offload your menagerie than it'd be worth."

"You've got that right, Fische. These damn xenobiologists are a pain in my keister! I don't know why you ever agreed to hire them."

"You'll have to trust me, Ernie. It was the path of least resistance." He had obviously never had to deal with an animal-rights activist.

"Whatever, Fische. So the meeting's on for Thursday?"

"Yes. We'll be arriving on Wednesday to set up security and make sure all the arrangements are set. I…uh…" I stuttered a little as Kik walked into the view behind Ernie's shoulder. "I'd like to request Turk as my personal security guard for the meeting, and I'd like to have Kik along as well, if she wants to go."

"Thanks, Harry!" Turk chimed from the sidelines, obviously delighted with the prospect of the duty.

Kik stopped in her tracks, turned to the viewer and asked, "Why me?"

Because I can't pass up an opportunity to have you dressed to the nines and on my arm, Kikira, my brain said inside my head. I just hoped none of it got out of my mouth.

"The opening meeting is a formal dinner, Kik. Aside from the fact that I thought you might enjoy a change of pace, I need an escort." And, yes, I managed to say that with a straight face. "But if you don't want to go…"

"Oh, no. I'll go. But I've got to do some shopping if it's formal."

"I'll have Gertrude put a car at your disposal. Take a trip to The Apple and pick out something nice. It's on me."

"Thanks, Harry," she said, and the smile on her wan features lit the dark little corners of my cynical heart.

Some of the joy had gone out of her job as pilot since there wasn't a lot of piloting for her to do with the new travel methods. Simply shifting the ship in and out of stringspace didn't challenge her skills much, so I thought the trip and a little socialization might perk her up.

And yes, I've still got a serious thing for my former pilot, but at least I'm coming to grips with my feelings. I'm also thinking of having Zook install my prosthetic brain in an alien body, just to see if I might get lucky, but what alien would I choose to be if I could be an alien?

What do you mean, pathetic? Just because I would change my body to attract a woman's attention? Come on; guys do it all the time. We go to the gym, get tattoos, pierce various portions of our anatomy—ouch—and even get hair removed or implanted, depending on the current fashion—double ouch. Maybe I could get him to put me in a Sheesharian body. That'd get her attention!

Okay, so maybe I'm a *little* pathetic.

"Don't mention it, Kik. Oh, and Turk, I'm having Zook work up something for you to wear, something appropriate for the occasion, with unobtrusive armament to match."

"Formal, huh? Whadaya mean, like I gotta wear a tux?"

"Think of a cross between a tux and powered battle armor. Think of it as a battle tux."

"Powered battle armor?" I'd made his day.

"I owe you a set from that little incident with the elevator on the *Limburger*. And with all the Sploig technology Zook's been tinkering with, I think you'll like it."

"*Sploig*-tech powered battle armor? Wow, Harry. I…I don't know what ta say." I thought he might break down and cry, or worse, try to reciprocate. Turk's idea of payback usually involves male bonding, complete with guns, girls, fast cars, violence, and police chases, so I intervened.

"Just say you'll keep my ass from getting shot full of holes and we're even."

"You got it, Harry."

"Oh, and Ernie, you'll have two more passengers besides myself. My assistant, Gertrude, will be organizing security at Apollo Station, and Zook will be upgrading the *Limburger's* systems with some Sploig technology just in case things get sticky."

"Zook! But isn't he—"

"Immortal and pregnant, yes to both." His face went back to mauve; another perk. "He'll need some space, so clear out the main hold for him. Oh, and I'll need Mishi to work up a special diet for him. I think spicy will be good for him. He's kinda bloated and has been a little constipated."

"Oh, like I really needed to know that! Thank you very much!" The screen went blank and I broke down into uncontrollable chortles. And yes, I'm sure they were chortles. I'd been practicing my chortles all week for this moment, and I got them exactly right.

***

The flight to the Moon was even less eventful than I'd planned. It seemed the *Limburger's* new captain had different ideas of how to run a stringship than I do. First, the crew were wearing actual uniforms, something I'd never cared for, especially when dealing with the Farfnians. The crabs don't like anyone other than themselves showing any kind of authority.

Second, he'd given Mishi quarters and made him sleep there instead of in the oven, which seemed rather silly to me since the thermostat in his quarters only went up to one hundred degrees, which was positively arctic for a Turpenoid. This left Mishi in a perpetual state of rage, and as a result, the quality of his cooking and the morale of the crew had suffered. Eating scrambled powdered eggs on toast three times a day will put anyone in a bad mood.

Third, and to my utter shock as I entered the bridge, he'd placed a privacy screen around the pilot's couch, complete with a little hanger for Kik's jumper. This would have seemed a valid addition if you didn't know Kik, which he obviously didn't. She's about as modest as the pope is Episcopalian. Her idea of privacy is remembering to put the "Ladies" sign on the shower door, which gives a whole new meaning to the phrase "good clean fun."

I sat down at the communications station and plugged myself in so we could talk during the flight. As we left the barn and gained altitude, I broke the ice with my usually suave repartee.

"So what's with the new furniture?" I asked, my mental voice transmitting into her auditory canals through the nanofibers of the pilot's interface.

"What? Who—" The *Limburger* yawed a bit. "Jesus, Harry! You scared me. I'm not used to someone talking to me while I'm flying." The ship resumed course, the mains kicking on full as we broke free of the atmosphere and made orbit. "You mean the screen? Ernie's just a little old-fashioned, I guess. He got a little uncomfortable without it."

"Uncomfortable?"

"He kept having to leave the bridge. Next thing I knew, he installed the screen and told me to stay decent. At first, I didn't know what he meant. I thought I was a pretty decent person, you know. I asked him, and he told me he meant clothed. Weird, huh?"

"Yeah, he's a strange one, all right."

I glanced at Ernie. I'd never really liked him much, and I knew how he felt about aliens. I'd even asked Zook to set up his toys in the main hold, out of everyone's way. Not just for our captain's benefit, though. Zook was starting to look even more alien than he really was. It was hard to find a jumper that fit him, and all his little bumps were turning a dark purple color that made him look like some kind of deformed anemone. If Ernie felt the same way about Kik, due to her xenophilic lifestyle, as he did about Zook, it would explain his discomfort.

Strange how it's hard to say "bigot" in a nice way, isn't it?

Anyway, I kept my temper and fostered a few fantasies about stuffing him into the airlock and hitting the purge button.

The trip only took about two hours. I can't imagine the old days when it used to take *days* to get to the Moon. I mean, what kind of propulsion did those old spaceships have, two guys on bicycles hooked up to a fusion turbine?

So Kik and I talked about nothing in particular, and I got a good sense of just how bored she was with the new setup. She didn't get to fly much anymore, just pop into stringspace and pop back out again on some distant planet. They got to meet a lot of aliens, since we use a lot of middlemen in the distribution of our product, but with the strict schedule there wasn't a lot of time for…uh…*fraternization*.

Hmmm, bored and lonely. The poor girl. My imagination enjoyed a few rounds with that until I got disgusted with myself and asked her the only thing that I really wanted to know.

"So, did you find something nice for the formal?"

I do *not* have a one-track mind! I have two tracks. Maybe three, if you count food. What can I say? I'm a slave to my urges.

"Oh, yeah, I found some nice stuff. Been a while since I had a reason to go shopping, let alone buy something nice. Thanks, Harry."

"My pleasure, Kik. I owe you for having to put up with Ernie."

"Yeah, you do. And don't think that one shopping spree and a nice dinner are going to make us even."

"Payback's a bitch, huh?"

"No, *I'm* a bitch. Payback is *dancing*."

"Dancing?" Now *I* was getting uncomfortable.

"Yes, dancing. I spoke to Gertrude, and she said she'd arranged for music."

"Great. Remind me to kill her when I get a chance."

"You're the one who wanted an escort." Amazing how her mirth came through the connection. "Now don't bother me for a few minutes. Reentries are tricky without atmosphere."

"Right. Well, have fun with it."

"Thanks, Harry."

I unplugged just as the *Limburger* did a flip and we started decelerating. I swallowed hard to keep my breakfast in place and smiled as Ernie let out an expletive.

"Tell her to give us some damned warning before she does that!" he snapped at Turk.

"Yes, sir." Turk sounded less than pleased with the order. I wondered if he'd broken any of his new captain's bones yet.

"Sorry, Ernie. I should have warned you. She told me we were getting ready for reentry."

"She told *you*? How the hell did she manage that?"

"Through this." I held up the wire that had until recently been plugged into the port in the back of my head.

"What the hell is that? I thought you were listening to music!"

"It's an interface into the ship's computer from my brain, *Captain*, and I'll thank you to keep your comments civil, unless you would rather be Turk's assistant security chief than captain?"

"Uh…yes, sir. Er, I mean no, sir. I'd rather be captain. I didn't know you had a… a…"

"There's a *lot* you don't know, Ernie. The sooner you accept that, the happier you *and* your crew will be." I got up as we touched down on Apollo Station's landing field and made a show out of moving the silly privacy curtain aside and helping Kik out of the couch and into her uniform, keeping my eyes firmly affixed to hers throughout. She grinned at her captain's discomfort, and I thought Turk would hurt himself holding back his laughter.

"Captain, please stay aboard your ship," I said, zipping her zipper and flashing her a wink. "Turk, Kik, and I need to check in to the hotel and get things squared away. Give Zook anything he needs, and I mean *anything*. You can contact me by comm unit if you feel the need."

Ernie stuttered something unintelligible and vaguely affirmative as I escorted my pilot and security chief to the lift. Turk, Kik, and I managed to keep our mirth in check until the lift doors closed, but then it broke loose and rattled around the inside of the tiny space all the way down three levels. It was good to be back.

CHAPTER FOUR

THE PALACE

The Palace de Luna is a big place; five hundred twenty floors big. This was good, since the addition of one hundred forty-three entourages from all over Earth might have otherwise raised a stir. They didn't even run short of bell hops.

You could have parked the *Limburger* in the lobby with room to spare. The floor is a single sheet of synthetic diamond, and the ceiling is the underside of a lake-sized plexicrete swimming pool. You could look up and watch guests plunge two hundred floors into the pool from their balconies, splashing into the water in slow motion.

Oh, you didn't know they don't use artificial gravity?

Well, that's the whole draw to the place, after all. You only weigh one sixth of your Earth-normal mass, and bouncing around in low gee is kind of fun, not to mention swimming, diving, flying—they rent wings—and doing lots of other things. Try shooting pool when the balls go flying off the table if you sneeze.

Anyway, the Palace swallowed our little meeting without even belching, so our anonymity remained secure. Gertrude had booked us a suite with four rooms and a view of the pool on the one hundred eightieth floor. As my assistant checked us in and the bell hops took our small mountain of luggage—most of it security equipment—I looked up and enjoyed the view of the swimmers.

"Did you bring your suit, Kik?"

"Suit? Her face showed only bewilderment. "No, I brought a *dress*, Harry. You said it was formal. I wouldn't wear a *suit* to a formal!"

"No, Kik." I pointed up at the pool. "Your *swim*suit."

"Swimsuit?" She looked up. "Oh, no, Harry. I didn't bring one."

"Oh." Okay, this is the way my mind works: I didn't know whether to ask if she didn't know the Palace had a pool, didn't swim, or simply didn't wear a swimsuit. I opened my mouth to see just how well my foot fit, when Gertrude delivered me from my impending oral ineptitude.

"You can go on up to the room, Harry. I'll see to the security setup."

"Good. Thanks, Gertrude." Then my brain did a little catching up, and I asked, "If you need some help, Turk's pretty good with security."

"No offense, Turk, but not with *this* kind of security. I'll be fine. You kids go and play." She adopted that mother-knows-best attitude that told me she could see through me like the plot of a bad murder mystery. She waved to her designated bell hop, and the little synthoid followed her away with nine-tenths of our luggage.

We only had two small suitcases, two suit carriers and my carry-on left. My brain did a little counting and I realized something was amiss: Turk and I both had suits and bags, and the carry-on was my work stuff, so where was Kik's luggage?

"Uh, you may want to grab Gertrude before she goes too far, Kik. I think your bags got mixed up with hers."

"Oh, no, Harry. I've got my bag right here." She lifted the wallet-sized purse she was carrying and smiled. "I travel light."

"I thought you said you bought a dress."

"In there," she quipped, dangling the purse and grinning.

"Uh, well, you might want another outfit for just walking around the—"

"In there."

"But what if we wanted to—"

"In there."

"What about accessories?"

"In there."

"Makeup?"

"Got it."

"Shoes?"

"Yep, in there, too."

"That must be some purse," Turk said, half of his eyebrow arching speculatively. Oh, I thought you knew Turk only had one eyebrow. It just happens to be over both eyes.

"Not really," Kik said, shrugging and following our synthoid bell hop toward the lift. "I just don't need much space, is all."

"All that and low maintenance, too," I muttered, following dutifully behind and trying to keep my fantasies in check. Yeah, good luck with that, Harry…

The ride to our floor was only slightly horrifying. You see, the elevator was glass.

I managed to face the closed doors for the trip and not let the view of people in bathing suits plummeting past in slow-motion disturb my delicate digestion. I don't know why these things bother me; I'm not acrophobic, and the view was really something, but the combination of motion, height, plummeting bodies, and no visible railing between myself and the drop left my knees shaking.

I started breathing again when the doors opened.

The suite was sweet—oh, come on, you knew I'd say it—with four bedrooms, two baths, a sauna, whirlpool bath, an entertainment center to rival Disney World™, a wide balcony and a springboard for diving. I decided to pass on the diving thing. Kik and Turk "Oo'd" and "Ah'd" like a couple of kids, checking out the mini-bar, the luxurious bathrooms and the entertainment amenities. I poured myself a scotch, kicked my feet up on the edge of the balcony, and checked my mail. Zook had upgraded my palm computer to interface with my brain, so I just sat there enjoying the view while I sorted through hundreds of letters, notices, announcements and advertisements for various male-enhancing drugs, surgeries, therapies, prosthetics, and transplants.

Amazing how our best technology can't eliminate the spam from my in-box.

"Turk and I are going to go find someplace nice for dinner, Harry. Wanna come along?"

I turned to tell Kik, "No thank you, I have work to do," but all that came out of my mouth was something like, "Wa waa wa, wa wa waa wa wa." You see, she'd changed out of her uniform into something…uh…well…something more Kik, and the input from my eyes was interfering with my brain's capacity to form words. I know my brain's a computer, and an Immortal computer at that, but any brain, cybernetic or organic, can only process so much before it goes "boink" and reverts to "wa wa" mode.

"What?"

"Oh, sorry, Kik. I just wasn't expecting your outfit to be so, uh... Well, it's kind of striking."

"You like it?" She did a little pirouette, and my brain did another hiccup.

"Uh...yeah, I like it." What was not to like? I certainly understood how it managed to fit into her micropurse with room to spare. "It's monolayer, isn't it?"

"Yeah! Feels like I'm not wearing anything at all!"

Well, with only one molecule between her skin and the rest of the world, that was easy to understand. The outfit hugged her from neck to toes like her own epidermis, and was colored with diagonal stripes of red, pink and white interspersed with clear bits. The light gravity didn't help. Light or no gravity does very interesting things to the female physique that cause the male brain to become flooded with enough testosterone to float a small battleship. Things just move when and where they shouldn't move, and in the wrong directions. Imagine a hundred pounds of incredibly sexy Jello™ belted to a random-orbital buffing machine.

Fortunately, my brain is immune to testosterone.

Yeah, right. And Earth Gov's president doesn't take bribes from the Farfnians.

"You look like a giant candy cane," Turk said.

"That's the idea," she countered, fixing him with a warning glare.

Turk's suggestion had my mouth watering for peppermint, so I thought it best if I just stayed put while Kik tortured the male population of the Moon.

"Thanks for the invite, Kik, but I've got work to do. Find someplace nice and pick me up for dinner."

"Okay, Harry. Don't work too hard!"

They left, and I noticed that Turk had changed out of his uniform, too, though I couldn't tell you what he was wearing. Isn't that strange?

Well, okay, maybe not.

If Kik's formalwear resembled her leisurewear, I was in trouble. I had a speech to give at this banquet, and even though memorization isn't a problem for me now that my brain is cybernetic, I do have to concentrate on what I'm saying. With Kik in the room that might be difficult, especially if she was dressed like that.

Maybe asking her along wasn't such a good idea after all.

***

Dinner that night turned out to be uneventful. Gertrude joined us and kept me busy enough to keep my mind off of my other dining companions—like that could happen. Nice place. Good food. I think Turk was there, too, but I really can't remember. Isn't that strange?

Security was all set. The grand ballroom was wired with enough scanning gear to read your Aunt Petunia's address from a slip of paper in your wallet without the inconvenience of you having to actually take your wallet out of your pocket.

Interesting how personal privacy takes a back seat to security when you're terrified, isn't it?

"Uh, these scans," Turk interrupted, his face twisting into a mask of worry. "Does everybody get scanned? Even us?"

"Well, it's only polite, Turk. I mean, they're our guests, and we're searching them; it only seems right that we let them search us."

"But what if I don't wanna get scanned?"

"Everybody gets scanned, Turk. If you don't, everyone will think you have something to hide." Gertrude looked at him like he was hiding something, which, of course, he was. "Do you have something to hide?"

"Well, maybe."

I knew what he was hiding, but I couldn't think of a way around him submitting to the scans without it appearing like we were trying to smuggle something in under the radar. "Can we keep the results of Turk's scans to ourselves, Gertrude? Turk's had some battle-related injuries best not viewed by the general public."

"You made the agreement with the others, Harry. They do their scans, and we do ours. Everybody gets scanned." She looked sideways at Turk. "What kind of battle-related injuries?"

"I was kinda…uh…" He lowered his voice to a faint rumble, "blown up."

"Blown up?" Gertrude's eyebrows shot toward her hairline, wrinkling up her forehead like a rug under the leg of a chair. "What do you mean? Like a balloon?"

"No, like an artillery round," Turk growled dangerously. "I had some prosthetics installed, and I don't want everybody to know, all right?"

"Well, everybody gets scanned. That's the rule."

"But we made the rule," I argued. "Can't we…bend it a little in this case?"

"No bending rules," Gertrude countered. "It's against the rules."

"But didn't we make that rule, too?"

"We can't go bending our own rules, Harry. What would it be like if everyone in power made rules that they could break any time they wanted?"

"Democracy?" Okay, that was a little cynical, I admit, but hey.

"Oh, stop it, you two." Kik broke up our verbal tennis match with her usual cool grasp of the obvious. "If he gets there early, and you scan him before anyone else gets there, he's in. If they ask, just tell them you scanned him, and that he's security, which is the truth."

Everyone looked at her as if she'd just sprouted a halo. I couldn't suppress a grin.

"All that and brains, too," I muttered, perhaps just barely loud enough for her to hear.

"Fine," Gertrude said, calling for the check before we could order dessert. "Get to the grand ballroom by four PM sharp, Turk, and I'll scan you in."

"And you won't tell anybody?"

"I won't tell a soul. I promise."

I didn't mention that I'd watched Gertrude promise all kinds of things, including the whereabouts of her boss, to all kinds of people, including her boss, without a shred of truth passing her lips. After all, what was the worst that could happen?

CHAPTER FIVE

CHEESEMOOT

I really ought not to ask that question, oughtn't I? As soon as I do, it's like calling down the wrath of the Gods.

On the upside, I got to hear Gertrude use a bad word.

It did upset me that her use of expletives was slightly more colorful than mine, but I'd never heard her use one before. Turk's insides displayed in living color—right down to every nut, bolt, circuit, and micropump—brought out the best in my administrative assistant, at least verbally.

"Holy (expletive deleted) on a Triscuit®, would you look at all the crap stuffed inside that boy!"

"Hey! You promised you wouldn't tell anybody!" Turk stepped out of the scanning booth and leveled a glare at Gertrude that would have sent Ghengis Kahn screaming for his mommy. He looked pretty imposing in his tux, kind of like a big black-and-white wall with a head. Of course this particular tux would have stopped a point-blank shot from an ion cannon, which took him up a notch or two on the intimidation scale.

Gertrude didn't seem to notice. She just kept expounding, saying things like, "He's got wires runnin' all through his head, and his heart looks like some kinda reactor core!"

"Gertrude!" My grip on her forearm finally stopped her, but the damage was done. The people setting up for the banquet had heard, and eyes were roaming over Turk like he had sprouted a spare head or something, which actually might have been a useful thing, considering his multi-tasking problem.

"Oh, sorry, Turk, but have you seen inside you lately? Who the hell did all this?"

"I *told* you I had a few prosthetics."

"A few? There's more metal than meat in there, boy! And what the hell is *that* thing! Oh, I'm sorry, that *is* original equipment."

"Hey! Why, I oughta—"

"Now, kids. Play nice, or I'll send you both to your rooms without supper." I didn't really think my little ploy would work, but I guess humiliation is a pretty sharp implement.

Both of them shut up and began studiously ignoring one another, but I could tell from one glance at the wait staff that rumors about Turk were flying around the room faster than water goblets and floral centerpieces.

"Forget it, Turk. Nobody heard but the wait staff. Just take up your station and watch the guests as they arrive. If we get a Sploig in this scanner, we're going to need some firepower, quick."

"Right, Harry," he said, flexing his neck with several audible pops as he glared at Gertrude and took station at one end of the scanning booth.

"Okay, you next, Harry," Gertrude said, giving me that "Yes, you" look that said "Yes, you" way more effectively than if she had simply said, "Yes, you."

I shut up and walked through the scanner. Gertrude knew about my little cranial implant, so there were no surprises or expletives to alert the room to my cyborgishness.

Yes, I *did* just make that word up; why do you ask?

Silly? Well, it's better than "strategic plan" or "precision estimate" or "preemptive first strike."

Anyway, we were early enough that I had a chance to take in the sheer grandeur of the Grand Ballroom. And let me tell you, they knew what they were doing when they named it.

The Grand Ballroom sits atop the tallest spire of the Palace, so it's got a pretty good view. At more than a mile above the surface, and with a dome of synthetic diamond giving us a three-hundred-sixty-degree view, I could see all there was to see of Apollo Station. Admittedly, that's not much, but the view of stars and the half-full Earth looming overhead made up for the lack of shrubbery in their landscaping.

I was trying to take it all in when a voice that I could not have expected less to hear broke my reverie. And yes, it was reverie. Starscapes do that to me.

"Turk?"

As you can imagine, with a broken reverie, I could only gape at the woman whose voice had broken it.

"Kely?" Turk answered, sounding like he had something broken as well. "I didn't recognize you! Whadaya doin' here?"

"Nice to see you too, Turk," she said, approaching my security officer like a tall, dark harbinger of…well…tall, dark musician-markswoman stuff. And I mean *tall* and *dark*. Kely was tall enough without heels, and wearing a long, black evening gown made her look like she was carved out of obsidian. Long sleeves and a high neck covered her tattoos, darn it, but that voice and her red-orange hair left little doubt.

"Uh, I didn't mean…I mean…well, I mean, what *are* you doin' here?"

I detected a note of suspicion in Turk's voice that made me proud. After so long in this game, and having been shot at by some of the oddest aliens in the galaxy, my level of paranoia could only be measured in terms of who I thought *wasn't* out to get me. It's a much shorter list than the converse. It was nice to see that Turk was running a close second. Neither of us much believed in coincidence anymore, especially when we'd both seen the Sploig up close and personal…and in my case, way *too* personal.

Which reminds me to ask Zook to program my brain not to have nightmares.

Yeah…

"The gig on Carpool got old, so I decided to come home for a while. I landed this one last week. They needed a violinist who wasn't afraid of low gravity. It can throw off your timing, you know." She stood about a foot in front of him and held out a hand. "Good to see you again, Turk. I like the look."

"I…uh…" He shook her hand, and I thought for a moment they weren't going to let go. "You look nice. I didn't recognize ya."

"Thanks," she said, amused by his faux pas. "Must be the dress."

"Yeah, that and no guitar or guns. You must feel naked without a piece."

"I little, but Ms. Mulberry told us this was a high-security gig. No problem."

"Oh, you mean Gertrude. I suppose she scanned you," he said, and I barely kept my jaw from dropping. Was Turk learning subtlety? I'd sooner have expected the Farfnian Prime Minister to walk through the door with a declaration of independence for Earth clutched in his claw.

"Right down to my DNA. She even made a comment about my ink-work."

"I suppose you heard what she said about my…uh…"

"Don't worry about it, Turk." She reached up and ran one long finger down the line of his lantern jaw, leaving a wake of rippling muscles. "Some women *like* scars."

He stood there like he'd been shot through the head as she turned and strolled back to where the octet was setting up.

"Uh, Turk?" I asked timidly. I was afraid to startle him at this point.

"Yeah, Harry?" He sounded a little stunned. Even more stunned than usual.

"I know this is kinda distracting, but you should watch the guests as they arrive, just in case. You know?"

"Oh, yeah, Harry. Sorry. I'm on it." He took up station at the scanning booth, but with the glazed look in his eyes I felt fairly sure he wouldn't be able to react in time even if we were attacked by a herd of club-wielding snails. On the other hand, taking his brain out of the loop might actually shorten his reaction time considerably.

I really shouldn't dis Turk in situations like this. He's never failed to react appropriately and in a timely manner when expediently blasting the crap out of something was required, whereas I tend to just stand and stare like an armadillo in the headlights.

"Your escort is here, Harry" Gertrude said, drawing my attention to the scanner as Kik flowed through.

Yes, flowed…

She flowed like space itself; a starscape of swirling galaxies, comets, and exploding nebulae came with her. Her monolayer gown displayed an ever-changing view of space, drawing my eyes like a magnet. She was covered from neck to fingertips, but it had to be the most sensuous article of clothing I'd ever seen on a human being.

"Close your mouth, Harry," she said as she extended one star-clad hand to me. "You look like an armadillo in the headlights."

See? I told you.

"Sorry, Kik, but that gown is…uh…wow." I took her hand and made a show of kissing it, which evened the score a little. "You really outdid yourself."

"You like it?" She did another one of her little pirouettes, which fanned out the lower portion of the gown and left me gaping again; the back was an open "V" from her shoulders to…well…far enough to remain decent, if only just.

"I like it very much," I managed to say without stumbling over my tongue.

"I'm glad. You paid for it, and it was terribly expensive."

"Worth every penny."

"What's a penny?"

"Never mind, Kikira. You look wonderful." I extended my arm and she took station beside me to help welcome our guests. WCC was footing the bill for this little soirée, so I was technically host.

Gilded guests started arriving in pairs and triplets—private security—and their finery dazzled even my jaded taste. I greeted them all by name and directed them to their prearranged tables from the seating chart in my head. Sometimes it's nice having a computer for a brain.

The music started, nice but not overpowering, and Turk started to fidget, either from the proximity of one who had so obviously won his amorous attention, or due to the fact that he hadn't had the opportunity to shoot anyone yet.

Ah, but the night was young.

When the last of the guests had arrived and, to my surprise and delight, none of them turned out to be Sploig, I seated my escort, then made my way to the dais where the band played unobtrusive chamber music. The music stopped and I addressed the crowd of almost five hundred, the perfect acoustics of the chamber carrying my voice to each and every one of them.

"Cheese Lords and Ladies, thank you for accepting my invitation to attend our little Cheesemoot." There were some mutters at this, some frowns, and some smiles.

"We have much to discuss, and rest assured, I will tell you all I know of the enemies we face and the technology we have discovered with which we may just prevail over those enemies, for the good of all."

More mutters, some clear enough to make out a few derisive terms like "altruistic" and "liberal". Someone might even have used that lowest cut of all, "socialist," but I paid no attention. I still held all the cards and everyone knew it.

I never really played cards much. It involves relying on one's luck, and mine's always been pretty crappy.

"But for tonight, please enjoy my hospitality. The food, I am told, is excellent, and the entertainment," I glanced over my shoulder at Kely and smiled, "comes highly recommended."

I bowed to my guests and said, "Enjoy!" The music started back up, and I made my way to my table. It was easy to find; Turk stood behind my chair like a tux-clad robosassin.

The food really was very good, and the wine even better. There were some other people at the table, and I said some stuff to them, I'm sure, but I really don't recall much of the meal.

Isn't that strange?

I couldn't keep my eyes off the swirling display of stars seated next to me. When dessert arrived, I finally had to ask.

"How does that dress work, Kik? The view keeps changing."

"There's a controller. I can pick any display I like, let it run randomly, or set it to change with my mood. It's pretty sophisticated. There are actually nanofibers on the inside, just like a pilot's couch, though not as many. It picks up my neural impulses."

"A very interesting dress." My mind started playing sordid little games, wondering what starscapes would be displayed under certain circumstances. I wonder sometimes if Zook programmed my brain to do things like this as a private little joke, or if it's my mind. And if it is my mind, how can a computer emulate all the quirks of a human psyche.

Quirks? Did I say quirks? How about intricacies? Yeah, I like that better.

I got a hint of just how sophisticated that dress really was when the waitstaff passed out a dark-chocolate raspberry torte with an accompanying old-vine Zinfandel the color of blood. Kik took a bite, and her dress swirled with the hues of a nebula. She followed the bite with a sip of wine, and a supernova exploded in the depths of that nebula, sending concentric rings of rainbow colors cascading across her curves.

"Interesting dress indeed," I said, sampling my own dessert. It was good, but hardly supernova worthy. I reserve my supernovas for special occasions.

Sometime during dessert, the music changed from that polite background stuff to a more pronounced beat that meant the meal was over and dancing was permitted. Kik's dress shifted from nebula to a pair of swirling spiral galaxies pirouetting around one another in perfect synchronicity.

I was in trouble.

I'm…uh…not much of a dancer. Oh, I know all the steps, thanks to a few learn-to-dance-in-ten-easy-steps programs I downloaded, but knowing it and doing it, I've discovered, are very different things. I wouldn't say that I have two left feet, but my right foot does seem to be slightly…uh…rhythmically impaired. Maybe there's a wiring glitch in my brain or something. Anyway, I was expecting Kik to tell me it was payback time any minute, so when Turk's baritone sounded in my ear in a stage whisper that probably carried around the entire room, it kind of startled me.

"You mind if I, uh…fraternize with the violinist, Harry?"

"Well, if security's tight, I don't see why not. Are we safe, Gertrude?"

"Locked down tight, Harry. Nobody gets in this place unless they can teleport, which Zook said he's monitoring for. If the Sploig try to pop in, we should get at least a few seconds warning."

"That's comforting." Well, it really wasn't, but there was nothing we could do to prevent teleports anyway. "Go ahead,

Turk." It would be worth it just to watch Turk dance with Kely. I hoped the floor was up to the strain.

"Thanks, Harry," he said.

As he weaved his way between the tables toward the tiny stage, I'll be damned if he didn't snag a rose from one of the floral arrangements in passing. Turk never struck me as the suave type, but I guess you don't get six ex-wives by being awkward with women. I have to admit, his timing was perfect. He presented the rose to Kely with a flourish and a little half bow just as the octet was finishing a waltz.

Kely took the rose with a sidelong smile, turned to whisper something to one of her musician companions, and put the rose between her teeth. The octet became a septet as she stepped off the low platform to the first thrumming notes of a tango.

Uh-oh, I thought, hearing the indrawn breath of my escort.

I'm not really the jealous type, but it plucked my pride like a poorly tuned piano to watch Turk and Kely. They moved like a single sensuous beast, stalking across the floor as if their feet never touched it. And out of the corner of my eye, I noticed Kik's dress erupting in a series of chain-reaction supernovae. I was in serious trouble.

Okay, so it's probably significantly less strenuous to dip a woman gracefully in one-sixth gee, but I knew that they were pulling off a serious triumph in managing to tango in reduced gravity. So much timing and rhythm depend on the effect of gravity. Don't believe me? Okay, do a pratfall. Oh, come on! You've got to know what a pratfall is! Now, how long did that take? Maybe two seconds, right? Well, at one-sixth gee, it would take about twelve seconds! That's a long time to fall when someone's waiting around to catch you, which is basically what a dip is, a pratfall with someone catching you at exactly the right moment. And since the tempo of the tango was not at one-sixth speed, Kely and Turk were *muscling* their way through the moves, instead of letting gravity have its way.

Doesn't sound so easy, does it?

What was worse was that they were making it *look* easy.

What was even *worse* than worse was the look on Kik's face.

Did I mention that I'm not the jealous type? And you believed that? Hmph. Go figure.

Anyway, I was studiously ignoring Kik in a vain attempt to avoid the inevitable, when my luck finally ran out. She reached one star-speckled arm out and relieved our table's floral centerpiece of one long-stemmed red rose. She then stood and held out a hand to me, which I dutifully filled with my own.

"It's payback time, Harry," she said, placing the rose in her teeth and pulling me to my feet.

I could not resist.

No, really, I couldn't. She literally pulled me out of my chair—remember the reduced gravity—and there was no way for me to remain seated, even if I'd been strapped down.

"You could have picked something easier than a tango, couldn't you?"

Okay, so if the glare she levied was any indication, my tone might have been a bit surly. Surly? Did I say surly? How about caustic or acidic, or better yet, downright acerbic. Yeah, that's it, I was acerbic!

"Tango is easy, Harry," she said, buffering my acerbicness with enough sheer feminine buffering power to pH balance the entire Venusian atmosphere. "All you've got to do is concentrate on the *rhythm*."

When Kik said the word "rhythm," every gland in my body suddenly surged with enough high-octane testosterone to overwhelm even a prosthetic brain. At that moment, I believed I *could* tango. And not only could I tango, I could tango the tango better than any tango had ever been tangoed, which proves exactly how clear my thought processes were working at that moment.

Fortunately, or maybe not so fortunately, as we stepped onto the dance floor, my comm unit bleeped and chirped in a poor imitation of Beethoven's Fifth Symphony. I had assigned that particular ditty to Zook—and no, I don't know why—so I stopped dead in my tracks and reached for the twittering little device.

"Don't you dare answer that," Kik said, leveling a glare at me that would have hulled a Farfnian cruiser.

"It's Zook," I said, as if that would get me out of my predicament. "He wouldn't call me unless it was important."

"Which means what?"

"Which means he's either giving birth or we're about to be attacked by aliens."

"Oh, well, okay. I guess you can take the call, then."

"Thanks." It gave me a warm feeling that Kik agreed that both of those particular forms of emergency rated higher than a tango. I pressed the "talk" button and said, "What's up, Zook?"

"Oh! Well, if you are asking for a definition of the word, up is the opposite of down, which is irrelevant in non-gravitationally influenced orientation, but if you are asking what is actually above me, well, the upper decks of the *Limburger*, a surprising amount of vacuum, and a Farfnian battle cruiser."

I'd been about to interrupt, when his last words brought me up short.

"A Farfnian battle cruiser?"

"Yes, Harry."

"Is that why you called me?"

"Yes, Harry."

"So, I can assume that they are headed this way?"

"Yes, Harry."

"Holy (expletive deleted)!"

"*Yes*, Harry."

"Keep this line open, Zook. We may need help."

"Oh, yes, Harry."

I turned to Kik, who had heard every word of the conversation, and shrugged. "Sorry, Kik, but we're about to be attacked by aliens."

"If I ever find out you planned this, I'll kick your nuts into a lunar orbit, Harry."

That sounded unpleasant, so I followed the tried-and-true practice of every politician and cheating husband in the galaxy: I denied it. "Planned an alien attack? Oh, come on, Kik!"

She would have said something, I'm sure, but that was when the entire Grand Ballroom started to vibrate with the subsonic thrum of a battle-cruiser's engines decelerating hard. A knife edge of shadow passed over the room, the glare of the sun blotted out by a huge black shape settling down over the transparent dome of our party. Zook was right; it was a Farfnian battle cruiser. Not just a patrol cruiser, or even an attack cruiser, but a mile-long, tetrahedron-shaped ship of the line. Astonishingly, it was not displaying the typically garish markings of a Farfnian military ship. In fact, it was painted flat black, without a single marking of identification or classification.

"This does not bode well at all," I said as a huge bay door opened above the Grand Ballroom.

The music died like a sparrow hitting a plate-glass window at full tilt. Everyone in the room stared wide-eyed with shock.

Consequently, in the utter silence, my voice reverberated quite well when I said, "Ladies and gentlemen, I think we've got a problem."

Yes, I *have* made understatement an art form; why do you ask?

CHAPTER SIX

TURK TIME

"Zook," I said into my comm unit.

"Yes, Harry?"

"Code Pepperjack."

"Yes, Harry. Oh, and thank you, Harry. This should prove most interesting."

"Just shut the (expletive deleted) up and do it, Zook!" Okay, so I was a little stressed. Two hundred thousand tons of Farfnian battle cruiser will do that to you.

"Yes, Harry."

The connection went dead.

I hoped that was the only thing that died.

"Ladies and gentlemen," I said in a voice loud enough to carry throughout the hall, "please proceed to the exits in an orderly manner."

Nobody moved.

I think they were a little stunned by the view.

The battle cruiser nestled down over the spire of the Grand Ballroom like a humongous mother chicken on top of a glittering diamond egg. The open bay would have engulfed half a dozen Grand Ballrooms.

Light erupted around us, a thousand blinding spears stabbing our eyes and making it impossible to see any details of the interior of the bay. Then a tubular shape snaked out of the shadows and attached itself to the transparent dome of the Grand Ballroom. It had teeth like a lamprey that spun up and engaged the indestructible—yeah, right—dome with a sound like ten thousand fingernails on slate.

If screams of panic were any indication, the corundum-tipped teeth eating through the barrier separating us from raw vacuum broke the armadillo-in-the-headlights moment much more effectively than my eloquent speech. People surged toward the single elevator like a herd of lemmings, oblivious to the fact that it would hold only about twenty very cozy humans at a time.

So much for the "orderly manner" part.

I take a small amount of pride in the fact that I was not one of the lemmings. Instead, I exercised my capacity as Big Cheese and escorted my escort to a cozy nook under a table. I'm not saying that hiding under a table exhibits more bravery than running in a panic toward an overstuffed elevator, but I *am* saying that it seemed more prudent at the time. I had the distinct impression that violence was about to break out.

How did I know this? I had a perfect view of the only two people in the room who weren't either running or hiding. Turk and Kely stood in a perfectly poised dip, unmoving and staring at the impending hull breech with rapt attention. Then they looked at each other…and smiled.

The teeth of the boarding tube breeched the dome, and a three-meter disk of synthetic diamond fell to the floor.

In the silence that ensued, Turk lifted Kely from their dip and tucked her behind his considerable bulk. "Stay close." He plucked at his sleeve, and a multihued shimmer of energy enveloped him. He flicked his wrists, and two small weapons extended from his sleeves into his hands.

"Got any spares?" she asked, reaching inside his jacket and grinning as she found what she was looking for.

Then the Farfnians flipped the switch.

If you're too young to have been on Earth when the Farfnians first visited, you probably don't know what I'm talking about. They have a device that interferes with electrical fields, disabling machines like computers, electric motors, generators, batteries, and all things controlled or powered by them. The term came to be known as "flipping the switch." As you might imagine, this was a subject of concern for me, having a computer for a brain. I had asked Zook about it, and he'd just chuckled that creepy Immortal chuckle of his and said, "Don't worry about it, Harry."

So I didn't worry about it. Much.

When the lights, the elevator, my comm unit, Kik's dress, and the band's sound system all suddenly went dead, I only felt a little lightheaded, but that was probably due to the sudden lack of opacity of Kik's dress. With its power off, the monolayer went transparent.

"Huh," she said, looking down at herself. "They must have flipped a switch. Your brain okay, Harry? You look a little stunned."

"I…uh…yeah. I'm okay, but it made my vision go wonky." Okay, lame excuse for staring, but I had to make *something* up.

"Looks like Turk's still up and running."

Sure enough, Turk's tux was still shimmering, and since he hadn't collapsed into a pile of spare parts, his prosthetics must have been as immune as mine. That was the good news. The bad news was that I no longer had a communications link to Zook. I knew that worrying about what he would do on his own initiative would drive me quickly into a screaming panic, so I tried to forget about it and concentrate on staying alive.

Over the years, I've discovered that there is always a moment of peculiar silence right before violence breaks out. It's like the universe decides to stop and watch or something. And knowing that all of stringspace is one giant sentient being makes me wonder if it might be doing just that. Well, this was that moment; it lasted no longer than a few seconds, but I could feel it building.

The Farfnians must have assumed that their switch killed all weapons of any consequence that we might have at our disposal.

They were horrifically wrong.

Five armored Farfnian marines swarmed into the Grand Ballroom through the boarding tube, dispersing in a perfectly executed pattern to cover every portion of the room. Four of them exploded in spectacular sprays of sizzling meat, armor and shattered weaponry as Turk and Kely brought their Sploig weapons to bear. One marine managed to get a shot off from his linguini blaster and even hit his target, but Turk's battle tux shrugged the single shot aside, and he sizzled the poor crab into a lump of slag before a second salvo could be fired.

Round one: crabs, zero; Turk and Co., five.

"Holy (expletive deleted) on a Triscuit®!"

I looked to the table beside ours to see Gertrude hunkered beneath, eyes wide.

"You okay, Gertrude?"

"I just…I mean he just…He (expletive deleted) *shot* 'em, Harry!"

"Well, I didn't think a *telegram* would have the same impact," Turk said, keeping his guns trained on the boarding tube.

"But they were Farfnians! He shot Farfnians!" Her eyes were so wide I thought they might pop, which would have been really icky, so I tried to calm her down.

"It's okay, Gertrude. They were bad Farfnians."

"Do you know how much *paperwork* results from shooting just one Farfnian, Harry?" If her tone kept climbing, our ceiling was going to crack. "And he shot *five* of 'em!"

"I think Gertrude's choo-choo has gone round the bend," Kik said, sympathy softening her tone.

"Besides, there's plenty more," Turk added, a grim smile stretching his caveman features.

"More?" I would have argued that even the crabs were not so stupid as to send more troops into such an obvious meat-grinder. Turk and Kely had an open field of fire, and the crabs had to enter a few at a time through a narrow space. It was like shooting fish in a barrel.

And who, exactly, would ever think to shoot fish in a barrel? Why not just tip the barrel over, pick up the fish, and have dinner?

Oh. Sorry. I digress.

Anyway, as much as I hate to admit it, Turk was right. The boarding tube flexed in the vacuum outside and a veritable flood of Farfnian marines spewed from the hole. Blue-white energy flared from their weapons, licking out to spatter against Turk's armored Armani® like bugs on a windshield. Turk and Kely poured on the fire, sizzling crabs into piles of scrap metal and cooked chitin as fast as they could come through. The carnage was horrible, the loss of life deplorable, and they just kept coming.

Only when the pile of parts threatened to fill the aperture did the parade of crabs cease.

"I think we need to plug that hole." Turk produced a small silver sphere, thumbed a switch and threw it right into the tube.

"Uh, Turk?" I hoped he hadn't just done what I thought he'd done.

"Yeah, Harry?"

"Was that a grenade?"

"Well, not exactly. More of a mine than a grenade, if you wanna get technical."

"But it's going to go *boom*, right?"

"Uh, yeah, Harry. Why?"

"Vacuum sucks, that's why."

"Oh. Yeah. I didn't think of—"

The charge detonated with a muffled crump, illuminating the shadows of the cavernous bay for an instant. My brain took a snapshot of that instant, and I didn't like the playback. I liked the sudden drop in atmospheric pressure and the gale that tore through the Grand Ballroom, sucking everything it could grab out through the hole cut by the Farfnian boarding tube, even less.

Including us.

"Hang on!" I yelled, taking my own advice and latching onto my table's central support, grateful that it was bolted to the deck.

Kik grabbed my leg, which might have been arousing if she weren't flapping in a hundred-KPH breeze like an incredibly sexy wind sock. At one-sixth Earth gravity, the wind was sweeping everything out the hole like a giant vacuum cleaner. Turk and Kely managed to grasp another table and were holding on. Gertrude was screaming a high-pitched wail of panic, slowly losing her grip, and I don't mean just on her weak grasp on reality.

At the moment before she let go, the air shimmered and a robosassin popped in right at her feet. She slid right into one of its tentacles, screaming in terror and surprise. Just as I started to shout exultations, it stepped over to us, its clawed feet crumpling the deck plates with every step, plucked Kik from my leg, shimmered, and vanished: pilot, administrative assistant, and all.

"Thanks, Zook!" I shouted into the thinning air as chairs, flowers, plates, musical instruments, and some of the other guests flew, slid, and tumbled past. Unfortunately, none of it was large enough to actually plug the hole.

What we needed was a really big cork.

I generally don't get good ideas in crisis situations; I leave that to people who specialize in crisis situations. I do tend to get lucky in crisis situations, which has bailed my bacon out of the fire more than once, but this time I had a bona fide good idea.

"Turk! The table!"

"What about the table?" he bellowed back at me, confusion written plainly on his blunt features. Okay, so my instructions could have been a little clearer. I tried again.

"Plug the hole with a table!"

"Oh! Right! Good idea!"

As he worked his feet into position to rip the table from its mounting bolts, I started to have second thoughts about my plan. I mean, Turk thought it was a good idea, right? As his powered battle tux strained against the table's mounting bolts, I saw realization dawn on Kely's face; the table was the only thing keeping them from tumbling through the hole into hard vacuum. But instead of abandoning said table and trying to find something else to hang onto, she clambered underneath it and helped him. As the bolts ripped free, Kely kicked the floor, flipping the table up to catch the maximum force of the wind. The two of them rode the table like a surfboard, right down the throat of the gale.

The instant before impact, they both kicked away in opposite directions, keeping the table on a perfect trajectory while they flew to safety.

I was impressed.

Then the table, Kely and Turk all hit the wall. Of the three, the table seemed to take the least damage from the impact, but it filled the hole nicely, and the gale-force winds ceased. Turk hit hard, but his armor took most of the impact, so when he fell to the floor at one-sixth gee, he managed to land on his feet and not fall over. Kely wasn't wearing armor, so her encounter with the dome knocked her pretty badly. She kind of stuck like a pancake thrown at a wall before she peeled away and fell.

And I'll be damned if Turk didn't actually catch her in his arms.

What a guy.

Considering that they were both still in formal wear, albeit somewhat rumpled, it was a very romantic moment, in a James Bond kind of way.

I clambered out from under my table just as Kely was regaining consciousness. It looked like she'd taken a pretty bad crack to the head. Turk held her very carefully, like she would break if he didn't, which she just might.

"I lost your guns," she said, blinking as if trying to focus on his face. "Those were good guns. Sorry."

"I've got more guns, Kely. Don't worry about that."

I guess they decided that their mutual love of firearms was enough to base a relationship upon, because the next moment they were kissing, and I was standing there feeling like a voyeur.

"I hate to break this up, but we're still losing atmosphere, and we don't have any power to run the elevator." Turk and Kely broke their clinch and stared at me like I was from another planet. "Hello. We're still in trouble?"

"Oh, yeah. Sorry, Harry." Turk put Kely down and she wobbled only slightly.

The Grand Ballroom was a wreck. A lot of the guests were sporting minor injuries and were obviously terrified, angry or both. Most of them were also looking at me, either hopefully or accusatively.

"Jhu arranged zis whole sing!" Jean-Verne said, trying to straighten his ruined jacket as he glared at me. "Jhu 'ave trapped us all 'ere for ze Farfnians!"

"I what?" I asked as the crowd looked at me like a skinhead at a bar mitzvah.

"Jhu are working for ze crabs!"

"Now wait a second," Turk said, stepping in front of me. I suddenly felt very secure, but I also didn't want my security officer to blast my fellow cheese lords into bits of charred meat.

"You're not making sense, Jean-Verne. Why would I kill a few dozen Farfnian marines if I planned this whole thing?"

"You did not kill zem. 'E did." He pointed to Turk and scowled. "Which is impossible. 'Ow did jhu kill zem? Ze Farfnians killed all ze power. Your weapons; zey should not work."

"And what exactly was that creature that materialized from nowhere, grabbed those two women, and vanished again without a trace?" Lord Colston pushed his way to the front of the crowd and wagged a finger at me. "I've never seen anything like that before."

"That's part of the technology that I plan to *share* with you all if we get out of here alive. Now help me figure out a way to seal that leak before all of our air goes away."

This, of course, was the cue for our pet robosassin to pop in right in front of me. Nice timing, Zook. A few of the cheese lords pointed weapons at it. Even though the weapons probably weren't functional, I decided it would be a bad thing if one nervous twit managed to kill everyone here by firing at the robosassin.

"Please do not point your guns at this nice robosassin," I said, stepping between it and the nervous crowd. "Turk, put your weapons away. We don't want it to get nervous."

"Vat did you call zat sing?" Jean-Verne asked as the robot held out one arm to hand me a shiny new comm unit.

"I called it a robosassin." I took the comm unit and keyed it on. "They are very advanced robot war-machines from a race of shapeshifters who want to steal the secret of cheese from us so they can take over the galaxy from the Farfnians. And they *don't* like being shot at."

"Oh. Vell. Zat is…uh…fine." Jean-Verne had either decided I was a loony or was trying to accept what I'd said and fit it into his picture of the universe.

Yeah. Good luck with that.

"What's going on, Zook?" I said into the comm.

"You are in trouble, Harry."

"You *think*? The Farfnians have attacked us, Turk shot up their assault group, atmosphere is leaking out of the room, the power's out, and now the other cheese lords are accusing *me* of setting the whole thing up. Tell me some *good* news, why don't you?"

"Well, you won't have to worry about the atmosphere leaking out."

"Why not?"

"Because the Farfnians are closing the bay doors, which will sever the spire and trap you inside their ship, which, I am assuming, they will pressurize to keep you alive."

The crowd rushed to the transparent wall and looked down. From their gasps of horror, I assumed that Zook was telling the truth.

"Well, at least they want us alive. That's some consolation. And the bad news?"

"I probably won't be able to teleport the robosassin in through their shields without modifying the *Limburger's* power systems, and right now I can only spare enough power to teleport him back with two more people."

"Okay. Well…" I looked at the crowd. "Who wants to go on a little trip?"

CHAPTER SEVEN

THE FARFNIAN AGENDA

"Take my wife! Please!"

I looked at Lord Colston as if he were joking, which he would have been if he'd been on stage with a microphone in his hand. Okay, it's an old joke, but I still laugh every time I hear it. I wasn't laughing now.

"We can only teleport two, and one of them, unfortunately, has to be Turk." My pronouncement caught several people off guard, not the least of whom was the Jersey Boy himself.

"No way, Harry! They'll cut you to pieces if I'm not here."

"Why him?" Colson asked, clutching his wife and looking a little pale. "Why not you?"

"First, we don't have time to discuss it. They want us alive, or they would have just shot off the top of the building. Second, we can't afford to let the crabs get hold of the technology in his gear. If they had weapons and armor like that, they'd be worse than they already are. And third, not me, because I really want to know who the hell is behind this. Okay?"

"What are jhu talking about, Fische? Ze crabs are behind zis! Who else could be?"

"Well, since this isn't a military ship and those weren't military assault troops, I'm betting some ambitious crab with a lot of resources is interested in cheese. That means he can be bargained with. That's why I'm staying. So who's going?"

After a few mutters of assent from the crowd, Jean-Verne stepped forward.

"We appreciate your candor, and your willingness to stay wiss us, Monsieur Fische. Send Lord Colston's wife. He spoke first."

"Fine." I turned to Turk. "Sorry, Turk, but it's got to be this way."

"I understand, Harry." He turned to Kely. "I wish I could leave you one of my guns, Kely, but we can't let the Farfnians get hold of it. I'm sorry you got messed up in this."

"I'm not," she said, grabbing the lapels of his tux and planting a very sincere smooch on his lips. "I'll see *you* later, Turk."

"Count on it."

And without a look back, Turk grabbed the terrified Lady Colston by the hand and told the robosassin, "Do it."

The robosassin wrapped one tentacle around Turk's heroically proportioned shoulders, and the three of them vanished.

"What a guy," Kely said, adjusting her mangled gown and fixing me with a glare. "If you get us killed after that, Harry, I'm never going to forgive you."

"Nobody else gets killed, Kely."

"The doors are closing!" someone shouted as the floor shook and started to tilt.

"Well, at least I *hope* nobody else gets killed," I said, trying to stay on my feet as the entire Grand Ballroom started to tip over. "Everyone run to higher ground!" I really don't know what I was thinking; I mean, the mass of a few hundred people, even at Earth gravity, wouldn't counterbalance a toppling building.

So you can imagine my surprise when, as we dashed to the high side of the room, the tilt stopped.

"Huh! How about that!"

"They're using towing cables, Harry," Kely said, pointing to the black blobs of molecular glue spattering against the outside of the dome. The Farfnians use cables like this to tow ships they've just shot to pieces; they're basically a glue ball at the end of an unbreakable cable.

By the time I could say, "I knew that," there were more than a dozen attached to the dome, holding us up like a ballroom chandelier. Then my comm unit crackled and Zook's static-distorted voice came through.

"We won't be able to talk… *static* …are up. There will be too much… *static* …to maintain contact."

"Zook! I can barely hear you! The doors are closed. Once their shields go up, we'll be cut off."

"Harry? I can... *static* ...too much static. We're following, but we're also having some... *static* ...installing it in the... *static* ...being a real pain, so Turk... *static* ...out the airlock."

That didn't sound good.

"Oh, and I'm having... *static* ...so it won't be long now!"

The connection devolved into nothing but static.

"Well, I think we're on our own for a while." I pocketed the comm unit and looked at Kely, but her eyes were focused over my shoulder, and were a little wider than should have been warranted by a breakdown in communications.

"I think we're in trouble, Harry," she said, pointing.

I turned to see a small robot hovering outside the dome. It had ten little clawed legs and a long, pointed nose with what looked like a drill bit at its tip.

"A breeching probe," I said.

"What the hell's a breeching probe?" she asked, giving me a worried glare.

"Watch," I told her, pointing as the thing's nose spun up and engaged the dome in a shower of dust and a sound like a thousand dentist drills doing root canals. "They're for breeching hulls without blowing the ship to bits. They usually use them when they want prisoners."

"Wonderful. But how does that thing take prisoners?"

"It doesn't." I pointed to the much larger craft settling into place where the boarding tube drifted in the low gravity. "That does."

"I don't get it. What's the breeching probe for, then?"

"It makes taking prisoners easer."

"Oh. And how does it do that?"

At that moment the breeching probe's needle nose pierced the dome and an even tinier proboscis poked through the hole. It sent a small puff of gas into the room, and just as I'd suspected, everyone collapsed into snoring heaps like it was naptime at Nana's house. Everyone, that is, but me.

"Well, that's interesting," I said to no one in particular, since they were all unconscious. "Must be a neuro-anesthetic."

I watched the other craft as it cleared away the debris of the ruined boarding tube, then matched an airlock with the hole cut in the side of the dome. The table fell away as the pressure equalized, and the airlock opened to admit another squad of very nervous Farfnian marines. Thankfully, they weren't so nervous that they shot me on sight. Honestly, considering our treatment of their comrades, I wouldn't have been surprised if they had. Seeing me standing when all of the others were flat out must have been a little surprising.

"Greetings, my good Farfnians," I said with a very slow and careful bow. Careful, because there were five humming linguini blasters pointed right at my chest. "Let me be the first to apologize for any previous misunderstandings that might have caused distress among you and your fellows."

"You are Harold Eugene Fische?" the squad leader asked, advancing until the muzzle of his weapon was right under my nose.

"Uh..." That he was asking for me by name was troubling enough. That he was obviously upset made it worse. Admitting my identity could be fatal at this point, but lying to an armed marine is not healthy either. I decided, probably for the first time in my life, that honesty would be the best tactic. "Yes, I'm Harry Fische."

"Are you armed?"

That answer was easier. "No, I have no weapons."

"Good. Follow me. Do not resist."

"Resistance would be futile. I will comply."

He didn't get the reference, but that wasn't surprising. Re-runs of Star Trek haven't quite made it big yet on the Farfnian black market, I guess.

CHAPTER EIGHT

CHEESE IS GOVERNMENT?

By the time the others started waking up, I was on my third scotch and my second Cuban cigar. Lonny MacAllen was the first to regain his faculties enough to pose an intelligent question.

"What the 'ell 'appened?"

He took in his surroundings; we were obviously aboard a ship, and a Farfnian one at that. What really peeled his blurry eyeballs was the opulently appointed table festooned with Earth delicacies of all types and descriptions, and me, enjoying a tumbler of Glenfiddich® and puffing on a stogie.

After taking it all in for a moment, he asked the next logical question. "What the bloody 'ell's goin' on, mate?"

"They knocked you all out. For some reason, I wasn't affected by the gas. You've been out for about an hour. We're in stringspace. Have a cigar." I indicated the humidors spaced around the table. Most of the others were rousing now, grunting and groaning like college kids after a frat party. Lord Colston let out a snort like a prize bull preparing to charge and sat bolt upright.

"Bloody hell! What?" He shook his head and blinked, looked around and took it all in. "Thought we were dead! Bloody crabs had us dead to rights." He reached for a bottle of Tanqueray® and poured himself a stiff drink.

I couldn't help making a face. I don't particularly care for gin; it reminds me of trimming my mother's juniper hedge as a kid.

"Good show, that, having that pet robot of yours whisk away my wife." He raised his glass to me and quaffed a healthy portion. "Ahh. First bit of gin to pass my lips in a fortnight! Bloody shrew."

Kely had stirred from her own chemically induced slumber and looked at him in surprise. “So you wanted her taken away so you could—”

“Have a moment’s peace without her yammering on in my ear, day and night. Quite right, my dear.” He polished off his drink and poured himself another. “So, what’s all this about, Fische?”

“You mean, why aren’t we dead?”

“And why did ze gas not affect jhu?” Jean-Verne asked, his narrow little eyes scrutinizing me.

“I have a prosthesis that must have interfered with the gas.” I puffed on my cigar and blew a smoke ring. “As to why we’re not dead, the only thing I can think of is that there is a very powerful Farfnian who wants to talk to us. All of us.”

“What I wanna know is how they found us out, ay?” Carol Brunte fixed me with a glare and pursed her mouth in the same accusative little scrinch that your mother uses when she finds out you’ve done something you shouldn’t have. “*Somebody* ratted us out to the crabs, ya know, and now we’re up to our armpits in ’em. I’d like to know who the rat is.”

“Jes, I too would like to know who among us is ze traitor.” Jean-Verne raked the group with his suspicious gaze. “Which one of jhu sold us out to ze rotten crabs?”

“Without delving into the melodramatic, I suggest you ask our most gracious host, which I’m sure won’t be necessary since they are undoubtedly *listening* to every word we say.” I gave Jean-Verne The Look and polished off my scotch. “So, is everybody up?”

A quick survey indicated that everyone was awake, though some were still suffering from the aftereffects of the gas. With all the formal finery, it looked like the morning after prom night, right down to the hangovers.

“Good. My guess is our host will make an appearance very soon.”

I really should have gone into theatre; my timing couldn’t have been better.

The door whisked aside and a short, rather frumpish crab with a mottled carapace and wearing the Farfnian equivalent of a grey flannel business suit entered the room. If he wasn’t exactly impressive, the two fully armored bodyguards flanking him made up for that lack. They toted enough weaponry to subdue a division of marines, or even give Turk a run for his money. Mr. Frumpy Crab took the one vacant seat at the head of the table, his guards at his shoulders.

"Welcome, my friends. I hope you have found the accommodations acceptable." He touched his pincers together and clapped his mandibles in a Farfnian smile.

"And jhu are?" Jean-Verne asked with all the smarm of a French waiter.

"Very pleased to meet you, Jean-Verne Routois. As I am all of you." Our host took a small metal box from a pocket, opened it and scooped out a tiny portion of fine yellow-white powder with the flattened tip of one claw. He held the claw under on nostril and inhaled sharply.

"Parmesan?" I asked.

His whole body gave a little shudder. "A weakness of mine. You will forgive me."

"So, jhu are obviously not wis ze Farfnian military. Why 'ave jhu gone to ze considerable expense of abducting us?"

"Abduction is such an ugly word, Monsieur Routois. I have *invited* you here to discuss recent changes in the distribution of your product." He made the box of cheese vanish into his clothes.

"And exactly what product is that?" Lord Colston asked as indignantly as only British royalty can.

"Please, Lord Colston, do not feign ignorance. I know exactly who you all are, what you do, and until a few months ago, how you did it." He waved a claw at the table of untouched delicacies. "This is why I have gone to such an expense to bring you all here together. We will discuss the recent changes you have made in the distribution of cheese."

"You could'a just sent out a bloody invitation, mate," Lonny muttered.

"I doubt any of you would have accepted a conventional invitation. I regret having to resort to such means, but with all of you in one place, I could not resist the opportunity to approach you collectively with a proposition."

"Which brings us to the question of how you found out the details of our little Cheesemoot." How our security had been compromised had occupied much of my thoughts for the last hour of watching my compatriots snore.

"I am not prepared to divulge my sources of information, Harry Fische. Divulging my sources will not be part of the aforementioned proposition."

He was starting to sound like a lawyer.

I don't particularly like lawyers.

"And if we choose to decline your proposition?"

"Even though, as Monsieur Routois astutely pointed out, I am not connected with the Farfnian military, I do have...*associates* in the highest levels of government. If you refuse my terms, you will be arrested, charged, tried, and incarcerated for the rest of your lives in a Farfnian detention facility."

He said "arrested, charged, tried, and incarcerated" like it was one word, which wasn't really surprising, considering the Farfnian justice system. They tend to expedite the process by doing away with all those pesky things like due process, fair and impartial representation, the Rule of Law, and the ridiculous notion that anyone is somehow innocent before proven guilty. Everyone is guilty of something. Farfnian prosecutors simply find out what it is and lock you up for it—forever.

"Well, at least that's better than being held as enemy combatants in the War on Cheese," I said, earning a few chuckles from my compatriots and a scowl from our host. "What exactly is your proposition?" I might as well know what I was going to tell him to stick up his cloaca.

"Your new distribution system is making mockery of interdiction efforts. You will abandon the practice immediately."

See? Now he was starting to piss me off. That lawyer attitude—all the "you will" stuff—just rubs me the wrong way. I figured I'd unload a little, just to break the tension.

"You're a cheese retailer," I said, pouring myself another scotch. "And you're losing money because our new distribution has cut into your profits."

"No. I am *the* cheese retailer, Harry Fische." He retrieved his little box and took another sniff of Parm. "And your new practice has done far more than cut into my profits, though that is true."

I smiled at my compatriots. This crab, however draconian in his techniques, was on our side. If the flow of cheese stopped, he would be out of a job.

"So the military is embarrassed because they can't catch us, and the government is embarrassed because the military is inept, and the populace has just about had enough of the ridiculous expenditure on the cheese war." I was beginning to see a light at the end of this tunnel. I didn't hear a train, so I thought I might just pursue it.

"That is essentially correct, but it goes much deeper." He tucked his little box away. "With our interdiction efforts even less effective than before, support to sustain the war has waned. This has affected the government's base funding adversely. Ending the war would be admitting defeat, which would lead to a change in government. Maintaining the war with nothing to show for the investment will strengthen political opposition."

"So, why don't you just win the war, mate?" Lonny MacAllen shrugged and picked a cigar from the humidor. He pulled a six-inch knife from the sleeve of his tux, cut the tip off of his stogie and proceeded to light it. "You obviously know awl abaat oua operations. This ship could wipe out every dairy on Earth all by its lonesome and end cheese production permanently."

There was quite a lot of uncomfortable shifting of position around the room, and a lot of glares in Lonny's direction, but he wasn't telling anyone anything that they didn't already know.

"Winning would be only slightly better than losing, Mister MacAllen, and would be much worse than even the currently unacceptable situation."

"Winning would be *bad*?" Okay, I was a little confused, which I will admit is pretty normal, but still… "How so?"

"If we bombed Earth into a ball of molten slag," he began, his mandibles clacking in suppressed aggression, "the Farfnian government would fall within a month."

"Well, that's reassuring, at least. But why?"

“Because, my dim-witted little human,” he pulled the silver box out of his coat and shook it for all to see, “in case you hadn’t noticed, Farfnians *like* cheese. The Farfnians who like cheese have money, and money is power. Imagine the backlash if we destroyed it utterly and forever.”

“So, jhu need us more zan we need jhu,” Jean Verne said, picking up on the idea that, despite our position as prisoners, we were not without power in this negotiation.

“Yes. As much as it pains me to admit it, we need you.”

A collective sigh of relief swept across the table like a wave at a sporting event.

“Not you individually, so do not think my threat to incarcerate you is empty, but we need cheese. Cheese is money, and money is power, and power is government. What government would destroy a commodity, legal or not, that can generate more revenue and political support than any *cause* ever invented?”

“So, by your definition, cheese is government.” I made a quizzical face. “Interesting. But you don’t control it, and that’s not acceptable to you.”

“We *do* control it. We *created* it.” His carapace flushed scarlet, a sure sign that his temper had gone from low to simmer.

“Well, I think a lot of cows would disagree with you on that one.” Okay, my smart-ass self was making itself impossible to ignore.

“Why do you think we pulled your insignificant little planet out of the gutter in the first place, Harold Eugene Fische? It isn’t because you smell good.” He took a deep breath and another pinch of Parm, which seemed to subdue his temper. “We recognized the potential of cheese before you did. We built this up from the bottom, and let you think it was your idea from the beginning. We even instigated and funded the Hindu Underground Bovine Cattle Advocacy Police to add a dangerous terrorist element, which showed all Farfnians just how unreasonable and dangerous humans really are. But now you’re breaking the rules, and we can’t have that”.

“Rules?” Lonny MacAllen poured himself a drink and grinned that goofy Aussie grin of his. “Wasn’t aware of any rules, mate.

From where I sit, your rules make about as much sense as tits on a wallaby."

Okay, that created such a vivid image in my head that I couldn't repress a chuckle, which many of my compatriots shared. I was beginning to like Lonny MacAllen's style. Our host, however, was not amused.

"From your miniscule perspective, that may be true, Mister MacAllen, but you all must adjust your way of thinking." He was trying very hard to keep his temper under control, which told me a lot about him. He wasn't used to being angered, and when he was, he wasn't used to having to control it. "There is an increasing lobby by the 'immoral majority' to *legalize* cheese, tax it, and make Earth a legitimate producer. This would devastate the Farfnian economy on many levels, and give the wrong message to a hundred other little dirtball worlds."

Eyebrows rose in unison around the table, including mine. There was the flash of gold, right there for every human in the room to see: Earth as a legitimate entity, not an occupied territorial province of the Farfnians. If cheese were legal, Earth would have a stake in the galactic market. That, everyone around the room realized, was the golden ring for Earth. The question now was: could we grab it?

"So, you want to keep cheese illegal, maintain your governmentally sponsored illegal activity, and keep up your marginally effective interdiction efforts to maintain political and economic support for a war you know you can win, but don't want to." That was my nutshell version. I've always been a nutshell kind of guy.

"Exactly."

"What's in it for us?" That was my 'nut' persona putting in its two cents worth.

"You get to remain free and continue to make obscene amounts of money producing and smuggling cheese. The status quo remains."

"Or we could just publicize the whole thing, turn you in, and lobby the Farfnian majority to pressure the government to legalize cheese." Okay, you might be thinking that I just tipped my hand, but I still had one very big card to play, one that I was betting my life—literally—that our Farfnian host knew nothing about.

Farfnian laughter is not particularly pleasing to the human ear, but is easy to recognize for what it is.

When his mirth subsided and he could speak again, he said, "Such naïveté. The government finds it useful and profitable to allow me to do business. I have, to date, received more pardons than I have appendages."

I'm *so* glad I made him happy.

"You have only one choice," he said, addressing the entire room. "Let us win a few battles and string the war along. You will all be rich beyond your wildest dreams, and no one will be the wiser.

"I'm already pretty rich," I said, puffing another smoke ring. "And my dreams are pretty wild." He had no idea.

"And what of ze Earth?" Jean-Verne asked, trumping me nicely.

"Earth remains what it is, a third-galaxy little dirt ball of no value at all except for cheese. That is essential for our operation to—"

"Essential for you," I interrupted, "not for us."

Pissing off Farfnians is usually not very healthy, but I'd had just about enough of always being the one who it's okay to piss off. Much better to be a pisser than a pissee, in my opinion, unless you're into that kinky stuff, which just seems a little icky to me, but to each his own, and if you're not really hurting anyone—Huh? Oh, sorry. Got sidetracked again.

Anyway, our host stood up and made a gesture to his two bodyguards, which elicited much manipulation of their weaponry and set their linguini humming, which was probably supposed to be scary.

"You have no options. What is essential for Earth is to remain the insignificant dirtball planet it is." He flushed a darker scarlet and clapped his mandibles in a Farfnian grin. "We are prepared to accept certain set-backs in our operation. It would be unfortunate if several humans were injured or killed in the abduction of known cheese smugglers."

"Yes, that would be unfortunate." I smiled back and blew another smoke ring. Time to play my card. "Especially since the last time you tried it you lost…uh… I'm sorry, how many of your shock troops were fried into charred meat when you attacked our peaceful little dinner dance?"

"Are you seriously threatening *me*?" His scarlet hue deepened to crimson, and a bit of drool spattered the table.

"No, I am making a point." I puffed my stogie and smiled to my compatriots, who were looking rather like a herd of deer on a six-lane freeway. "You supposedly deactivated all of our weapons, then proceeded to get slaughtered by only two of my security people, who didn't even get a scratch themselves. We are not as toothless as you presume, my good Farfnian. We have changed more than our delivery techniques, and have discovered a few gadgets that don't seem to be affected by your dampening field."

"This human is *not* helping your case," he said to the others, waving a claw at me, which sent his two goons forward. They jerked me out of my seat and started for the exit. "He is being threatening and unreasonable, and will be excluded from our agreement."

"We also discovered an enemy you don't even know you have," I said over my shoulder. "One that wants to break the Farfnian hold on the galaxy and regain control for itself."

"*Regain* control? What are you talking about?" he said, stopping my escort in their tracks.

"He's talking about the Sploig," Kely chimed in, right on cue.

Me doing all the talking was getting a little old, not to mention encouraging our host to delete the troublesome one—me—and negotiate with the rest. This would have been very bad, since my compatriots knew nothing of the Sploig, their technology, or their plans to take over the galaxy.

"The what?"

"I guess you don't have all the answers after all. How about that?" Satisfied smirk? Damn right!

CHAPTER NINE

I SEE YOUR EARTH AND RAISE YOU A SPLOIG

"The Sploig are more of a who than a what," I said as the grips on my arms eased enough for my feet to touch the deck. "They're the ones who stole Tillamook."

That line is always such a crowd pleaser.

I hoped Mr. Frumpy Crab couldn't read human expressions as well as I could read his. The entire room looked like they had just found a very large bug in their soup.

"*We* destroyed Tillamook," our host said, his hue shifting to a mottled brown. He was worried, which was good. At least I hoped it was good. It was good if he wasn't the type to solve his worries with a gun.

"Yes, you did, *after* it was stolen by the Sploig and taken to their home world, where we tracked it down and returned it." I sat back down, retrieved my fallen stogie, and puffed it back to life. "Even ENN had trouble explaining why you dropped an asteroid on a cheese factory that had vanished a week before. You really should see the Sploig home world, by the way. It's very impressive."

"You are lying to save your own life, Mister Fische. The Farfnian Empire has ruled the galaxy for five thousand years."

You know, that's one thing that never ceases to amaze me. People—and I mean all people, both alien and human—seem to think in terms of their own temporal perspective. Humans think a hundred or two hundred years is a long time, whereas Turpenoids think of three or four hundred years the same way. We think a civilization that has lasted five or ten thousand years is venerable. Now, consider the perspective of the geologic time of a simple planet being in the realm of millions or even billions of years. A planet like the Earth is a few billon years old. A middle-aged solar system might be five billion years old. A galaxy? Maybe ten billon. If you think in those terms, a measly five thousand years is a blink of an eye.

"And the Sploig ruled it for the previous hundred millennia, give or take a few." I poured myself another scotch and sipped, enjoying the smooth single malt while my host's carapace shifted colors a few times. "Oh, and they kinda want it back."

"Explain to me then, Mister Fische, why I have never heard of these Sploig?"

"Because they didn't *want* you or anyone else to know about them. They run things from behind the scenes, remaining anonymous and hidden. And they are very good at remaining hidden."

"A race that ruled the galaxy for a hundred thousand years could not have remained anonymous!" He took another pinch of Parmesan. His claw was shaking slightly.

"Let me put it this way." I glanced around the room and cocked an eyebrow at my host. "There could be half a dozen in this room right now and you wouldn't know it. We checked everyone at the party, but that doesn't mean we didn't miss a few."

"Ridiculous!"

"Not so when you consider that the Sploig are shapeshifters."

"You mean like the legendary Immortals? Another myth!"

"Immortals are mimics, not shapeshifters, and my engineer Zook is anything but mythical. I've seen Sploig shift shape right before my eyes. They can take the shape of anyone or anything you can name, right down to sweat, smell and, uh…social interaction." I swallowed hard, trying not to recall all those nights with the Sploig that stole my heart and used it for a punching bag.

"They're also communal. Four of them can make up a human being. It'd probably take six to make a Farfnian, and it takes eight to make a Carpoolian. The more of them that join together, the smarter they get, and their world is nothing but one singular, interactive, cooperative organism of individual shape-shifting sub-organisms all thinking as one. And what they're thinking is how to get their galaxy back and still stay hidden from every other sentient species in it."

Nice speech, if I do say so myself. It certainly shut up the opposition, but I couldn't tell if they were in awe, struck dumb with the enormity of the truth, or thought I was a raving loony. In retrospect, I know they thought I was a raving loony, but I really must have been living right and paying all my taxes, because that particular moment was when all the deities in the universe suddenly smiled down at me.

My comm beeped in the tinny tones of Beethoven's Fifth Symphony.

It was Zook.

"And the answer they've come up with," I said, taking my comm out of my pocket, "is cheese." I clicked my comm on and answered, "Yeah, Zook, what's up?"

"We are in stringspace," Mr. Frumpy Crab interrupted, shifting to an altogether new shade of mottled mauve that would have looked great on a couch. "Your communications device should not be working."

"Oh, did I not mention that we juiced up our technology with some Sploig bits and bobs? Their tech kind of makes yours look like an ant farm, by the way. Zook? You there?"

"Uh, no, Harry. Zook's a little busy. It's me. Turk."

My insides went cold. I'd just drawn to an inside royal flush and gotten the duce of clubs. But if there's one thing I've learned in this game, it's how to switch from "win" mode to "bluff" mode in the bat of an eyelash.

"Great, Turk. H-how's the ship?" My voice was upbeat; perky even. Uh-huh. Well, I was trying for perky, but probably sounded more like Porky. The entire room was still staring at me. I just smiled and nodded, holding up one finger in that universal sign that I would only be a minute.

"The ship's good, Harry. Zook made some improvements. We're right behind you."

"Good! And Ernie? Is he there?"

"Uh, no, Harry. He got a little outta hand when Zook started adding the new systems. We had to…uh…convince him to stay in his quarters."

"And Kik? Is she there?"

"No, Harry. She's helping Zook. He's having…uh…well, he's having some problems."

"Okay. That's fine. Wh-who's pa-piloting the sha-ship?" Yep, definitely going into Porky mode.

"Oh, Gertrude's piloting, and Lady Colston's working the tactical board. Who knew your secretary could pilot a stringship? The pilot's couch was a tight fit, though. I had to sit on the lid to get it to close."

"Oh. Good." A wave of nausea accompanied the visual image of Gertrude getting into the pilot's couch. "Say, Turk, would you mind sending over our Sploig friend?"

"Sure, Harry. I'll just have it home in on your signal. Hang on."

"Thanks, Turk."

The comm unit went silent. Everyone in the room was still staring at me, probably convinced that I'd slipped a cog, blown a gasket, or otherwise glitched my CPU. Despite all the setbacks, I still thought I had a pretty good play going on; at least, I would if Turk could deliver.

I didn't feel so good about depending on Turk in a situation that required something more than blasting the (expletive deleted) out of something, but I didn't have much choice, did I?

"We're going to be having some company," I said, in my best please-believe-that-I-am-not-a-raving-lunatic voice. "Please encourage your security guards not to get trigger-happy."

"Company? What do you mean? We are in stringspace, traveling on a string with our shields up. Nobody is coming aboard this ship!"

Our pet robosassin materialized with a shimmer right beside me, right on cue. You'd almost have thought that I'd planned it. Good Turk.

The two bodyguards reacted predictably, training their weapons on the thing and moving to protect their boss. The robosassin reacted as its base programming demanded and pointed three of its six arms at the Farfnians. If anyone fired, the entire ship could be blown right out of stringspace, us along with it.

"Don't shoot!" I don't know if I was talking to the robosassin or the crabs, but it seemed like a good thing to say, even if nobody was paying attention to me. If things went badly, I could always say I tried, right?

"Hold your fire," Mr. Frumpy Crab said and his bodyguards seemed to take heed. At least they didn't fire, which saved their lives. "What is this thing, Mr. Fische?"

"This is a piece of Sploig technology that we managed to steal during our last encounter. It's called a robosassin. They use it to eliminate members of their own species who threaten the secrecy of their race." I smiled at my host with a little more confidence. He couldn't call me a lunatic now!

"You are insane!"

Okay, so maybe I was wrong. He *could* call me crazy, but he really didn't mean it; he was scared out of his carapace and in denial of what his own six eyes were telling him.

"No, he is not," Lord Colston interrupted, coming to my aid. "These things can perform feats that your technology could never accomplish. His two security guards, armed and armored with this Sploig technology, stood against an entire platoon of your best shock troops and didn't get a scratch," he reminded our host.

"Their vehicles and ships are armed and armored the same, and they can teleport, as you saw, right through your shields." That actually might have been one of Zook's Immortal tricks, but I wasn't going to let our host in on that little gem.

Mr. Frumpy Crab was starting to fade to a dull grey, the hue of defeat. He fumbled for his little box of Parmesan, but his pincers were shaking so badly that it fell to the deck and rolled past his bodyguards' clawed boots into the space between the armed opponents. I stepped forward and picked up the little round container.

"You're lucky the Sploig don't like open warfare. If they did, we'd all be in trouble." I held out the box. "You're also lucky we got to you before the Sploig infiltrated your operation and took control."

That, of course, was the cue for one of my host's bodyguards to point his weapon at me and say, "You are too late, Captain Fische."

"Oh, crap."

I actually watched the thing's clawed hand flex within the mass of noodles that would send a stream of fusion plasma lancing right through me. I cringed as light flooded the room. Something hit me, but without much impact. The light faded, and I looked down. My tux was scintillating with rainbow hues, shedding the energy it had just absorbed from the Sploig's linguini blaster. I adjusted my cufflinks and smiled a predatory smile.

"Bloody *smashing* tuxedo," Lord Colston said, his voice brimming with envy.

"I'll introduce you to my tailor," I said, keeping my eyes on the Sploig. "Robosassin, please kill the Sploig."

Even before the last word was out of my mouth, the Sploig started to fall apart, but robosassins are quick and can shoot six weapons at once, each at a different target. Only one missed, and that Sploig skittered across the table, scattering delicacies in all directions. The other Farfnian bodyguard fired and the middle of the table exploded, sending pâté de foie gras, crab claws, caviar, and bits of Sploig spraying in all directions.

When the smoke cleared, Mr. Frumpy Crab snatched the tiny box out of my hand, ripped the lid off and knocked back its entire contents in one snort.

"Believe me now?" I asked, recovering my scotch and following his example. "See what you're up against?"

"If they could impersonate one of my personal guards, they could…" The silver box clattered to the deck from his numb claw. "We have been infiltrated!"

"No, you've been Sploiged." I tossed my empty tumbler onto the ruined table. "Join the club."

He turned to his other guard and said, "Sound the general alarm immediately. Intruder alert. Full security stations!"

"Wait!" I held up a hand, and I'll be damned if they both didn't stop and look at me. Ha! I guess I'd gained a little credibility in the last sixty seconds. "If you send out a general alarm, you're telling every Sploig on the ship that you're hunting them. They'll vanish, and you'll never find them. There could still be more in this room for all you know."

"So, how do we fight them, Mr. Fische?"

"I can tell you how to smoke them out, but we've still got some negotiations to complete." I puffed my stogie to life and blew a smoke ring, a *perfect* smoke ring.

"We cannot negotiate while there are intruders on this ship!" Mr. Frumpy Crab insisted, waving his claws for emphasis.

"Well, right now, you're outnumbered," I smiled over my shoulder at my cohorts, most of whom were still staring in shock at the crater in the middle of the table, "outgunned," I nodded to my robosassin companion, "and need my help to rid you of a dangerous infestation of Sploig." I puffed again and blew another ring right into his mandibles. "From my position, it's the *perfect* time to negotiate."

"What do you want, Mr. Fische?" he said, slurring his words with all the hate a crab can muster, and let me tell you, when it comes to hate-mustering, crabs are pros.

But when it comes to haggling, humans have them beat hands—and claws—down.

"Well, let's start with an independent planetary charter for Earth and work up from there, shall we?"

I was very pleased with his sputtering response.

CHAPTER TEN

UNKA FISCHIE

Bringing everyone back to the *Limburger* wasn't as taxing as I thought it would be. The robosassin made a few trips, daisy-chaining with about fifty of us at a time. I didn't think it could do that, but when I got back I found out how it had managed such a seemingly impossible feat.

"Zook's upgraded the *Limburger* with some Sploig technology," Turk explained, standing up from the captain's couch as Kely and I stepped onto the bridge. A few dozen wires disconnected from his neck and reeled back into the seat. "He added a few Immortal gizmos, too, but said he'd better stop before the computer woke up."

"Woke up?"

"Yeah. You know, became conscious or self-aware or whatever." He stepped over to the tactical station and said, "I'll take over now, Lady Colston. Thanks for the help."

"My pleasure, young man." Lady Colston stood and smiled at Turk, dusted off her evening gown and turned to me. "And where, may I ask, is my husband? Probably out drinking and womanizing, if I know him!" She glared at Kely for a second, but I intervened before things got nasty.

"He's in the main crew mess with most of the rest of the guests. We were stretched a little thin for elbow room, so some of them are in the main hold." I ushered her to the lift. "Your husband was a big help negotiating with the Farfnians. He's a natural."

"A natural boor," she said, unconvinced. She exited the bridge without even a thank you. Hmph…*royalty*.

“Well, at least we managed to—” My brain got stuck as I turned around and saw that Kely and Turk were happy to see each other. Very happy.

“Ah-hem?”

No response. Make that *ecstatic* to see each other.

“Um, Turk? I’m sorry to break this up, but we’ve got to turn the ship around.”

Still nothing. How about lip-locked-and-all-but-ripping-each-other’s-clothes-off happy. I figured I’d better interrupt before things went too far and I had permanent eyeball damage.

“Turk! Kely! Knock it off! We’ve got stuff to do!”

“Oh, sorry, Harry,” they both said, then looked at each other and grinned that goofy in-love grin that I knew all too well.

Damn Sploig…

“Kely, if you could take the communications board, and with Turk on tactical, we’ll see what we can do about turning this—”

That was when the pilot’s couch sprang open and my eyes were burned to little lumps of charred vitreous humor right in their sockets. Well, okay, not really, but it felt like it. I closed them as quickly as possible, but the image was indelibly burned into my infallible memory. At that point, I wished my memory was a bit more fallible.

“Oh, stop it and help me outta this damned thing, Harry.”

“I…uh…” I opened my eyes for a second, but they closed automatically. It was like trying to look into the sun. “I can’t. Sexual harassment laws, you know.”

“I’ll help,” Kely said, rescuing me from a fate I could not have endured without a post-traumatic memory wipe.

If you can imagine a sound like a hundred balloon animals stampeding across a leather armchair, that’s kind of what it sounded like as Kely helped extricate Gertrude from the pilot’s couch. The stampede ceased, to be replaced by muffled grunts and curses that could only mean Gertrude was struggling back into her evening gown. I kept my eyes closed just to be safe. When the curses eased off, I risked a peek.

The last zipper was zipped; my eyeballs were safe again. She did, though, look a little goofy without hair.

"I must say, Gertrude, I didn't expect you to…uh… Well, I didn't know you could pilot a ship."

"It's not something I put on my resume," she said with a little shimmy that straightened her gown and almost knocked the ship right out of stringspace. "I gave it up when I had kids, though; they don't make pilot's couches in my size."

"Well, thanks for stepping up to bat." I sat in the captain's chair and experienced a rush of nostalgia. Oh, for the days of being a simple cheese runner… "I hate to ask, but you might have to squeeze back in there if Kik's not able to take over."

"I'd really rather not, unless it's an emergency. That couch was pinchin' off my circulation."

"No rush. The Farfnians will be chasing Sploig for a few hours, at least."

I leaned back, got comfortable, and took a second to glance at the new controls under the armrests. Some were labeled with Immortal symbols. Since I was probably the only human in the galaxy who could read them, Zook must have put them there for me. One of them was labeled in red symbols: "Harry: Do NOT push this button!" Yep, they were for me all right.

Gertrude sat down at the engineering station and looked over the board. "Man! Zook really went to town on this baby. Flying her was like a roller-coaster ride on fast forward."

"Oh, I forgot to mention, Harry, Zook rigged the captain's chair to interface with—"

As Turk spoke, I felt a tickle at the back of my neck. Something clicked into the socket Zook had installed in my skull, and a sultry feminine voice said, *Hello, Harry,* in my head.

"Someone's talking in my head, Turk." It felt the same as when I spoke with Kik through the pilot's interface, but there was nobody in the pilot's couch. "Why is someone talking in my head?"

"That's what I was tryin' to tell you. Zook upgraded the captain's chair to interface the computer with anyone who's got the hardware. As far as I know, that's just you and me." He smiled one of his Cro-Magnon smiles. "Guess we've got somethin' in common."

"Great!" Strangely, having one more thing in common with Turk was not the highlight of my day. "And why does it sound female?"

"You'll have to ask Zook that one. Maybe it's a girl because it wants to be a girl."

"But I thought you said it wasn't self-aware."

That's not a very nice thing to say, it said in my head.

"It sure sounds self-aware."

"It's not, but it simulates a personality pretty good, doesn't it?" He gave a little twitch, like something was tickling the back of his neck. "Kinda creepy, huh?"

"Sounds like a person, to me."

Thank you, Harry. That's the nicest thing anyone's ever said to me.

"You're welcome," I said.

"Huh?" Turk looked at me like I was talking to him, and I realized I'd spoken aloud.

"Sorry, Turk. I'm talking to the computer. Carrying on two conversations at once is a little confusing." Mentally, I said, *So, what do I call you?*

You don't have to call me anything, Harry. I don't really have a name. The tone in my head sounded a little forlorn. I had to remind myself it was a computer. But, then again, technically so am I.

Well, I've got to call you something. Lots of people have voice-interactive computers, and most of them name their computers to limit confusion when they're interacting with them. *Tell you what, scan my memory and pick out a nice name, something that won't be confused with any of the crew's names.*

How about Daisy? it said after about a half-second. It either found what it wanted early in its search, or my memory's not all that deep.

Daisy? I'd had a dog named Daisy when I was a kid, a mixed-breed little mutt that drove my mom crazy by systematically chewing every item in the house within reach. *Perfect. Just don't start chewing up shoes, okay?*

Daisy gave a little giggle in my head that made it really hard to think of it as nothing but a bunch of wires, chips and circuit boards.

"Turk, the computer has chosen a name. Enter 'Daisy' into the ship's register, and list her as 'AI Specialist'."

He looked at me like I'd asked him to paint himself blue. "Uh, okay, Harry, but why?"

"Because every crewmember deserves a name and designation, and I can't very well call her 'Computer'; it sounds stupid."

Crewmember? Daisy said, elated. *Oh, thank you, Harry!*

"Crewmember?" Turk asked. "The computer's a crewmember?"

"Yes, Turk, and her name is Daisy, so get used to it."

"The computer's name is Daisy?"

"Kik!" Everyone turned as our pilot exited the lift. "How's Zook?"

"He'll live, but he's kinda beaten up." She took a step and did a little half-stumble, leaned on the tactical console and shook her head. Turk was on his feet in a second and steadied her.

"You okay?" he said, motioning Kely over.

"Sorry, I'm a little lightheaded. Zook's kids are, well..." She looked back at the lift and said, "Why don't you all just come out and tell him yourselves?"

"Who..." I hadn't noticed anyone else on the lift, so when two more Kiks, two Mishis and two Charlies stepped out like clowns from a tiny circus car, my jaw dropped like the stock market the day after the Farfnians landed. "What the..."

"These are some of Zook's kids." She smiled and motioned them forward. "Come on, you can come in."

They edged forward, looking around like, well, like kids in a new environment, which is what they were, despite the fact that they looked like three pair of twins of my crew members.

"They learn really fast, and Zook said it would be best if we showed them around the ship. Charlie took a few down to the hold, and Mishi went to the galley with a few more."

"More?" I asked, eying the twin versions of Kik. I sat back down in the captain's chair and casually crossed my legs. "Uh, how many more?"

"I think there are sixteen, but there might be a couple I missed. One mimicked a piece of furniture, and another ended up as an avocado until Zook coaxed them into picking other forms." She smiled at the six apparently newborn Immortals and said, "It's okay. Come in and meet your uncles. This is Harry, and this is Turk. And these are your aunts, Kely and Gertrude."

"I am *not* an aunt to that weirdo's kids, Kikira." Gertrude glared so hard that the six lost their smiles and cowered behind Kik, which was almost comical.

"Okay, so Gertrude isn't the nicest human on the ship," Kik said with a glare of her own, "but she won't hurt you. Harry has known Zook longer than anyone."

"Harry Fische?" one of the two Mishis asked, eying me with an odd expression on its ruddy Turpenoid features.

"Yes, I'm Harry Fische." Well, what was I *supposed* to say?

"Unka Fischie!" they all said, rushing forward, hands outstretched. This worried me on three counts: first, I was outnumbered; second, I had no idea if they were dangerous or not; and third, Turpenoids are *hot*.

"Ouch! Hey, Kik, get the—" Having a Turpenoid hug your leg is not something I would suggest as a recreational activity, unless you are into pain. Fortunately, the three of Zook's kids who managed to get a good grip on me immediately let go. But, to my utter flabbergastedness—is so a word—they fell to the floor and started quivering like the possessed at an exorcism. "What the hell?"

"Uh-oh." Kik stepped in, urging the other three away, but one copy of each pair lay there writhing like they were having seizures. "Sorry, Harry, but they're all a little morph-happy. Zook said it's just something Immortal kids do."

"Morph-happy? Oh, no. You don't mean…" The next thing I knew, the flesh of all three of them shifted and ran like melting wax, and there were three copies of me getting up from the deck and looking down at themselves as if checking out a new suit of clothes. This would have been uncomfortable, even if the one who had previously copied Mishi wasn't naked.

"Turk, could you scare up a spare jumper for that one, please?"

"Sure, Harry," he said, amid the chortles of the rest of the crew.

"Actually," I said, a thought coalescing in my mind, "having a few copies of myself might not be a bad idea right now."

"You just want someone to sit in on meetings for you," Gertrude said, proving once again that she knew me far too well.

"Well, *yeah*, but I was also thinking of all the things that are going to hit the fan in about a week, and all of the people who might not like me for arranging it all." Turk and I helped the me-copy who was clothing challenged into a spare jumper.

"What exactly happened over there, Harry?" Gertrude asked, scowling again. "You said the Farfnians would be chasing Sploig for a few hours. I'm assuming their ship was infested?"

"Like ants at a picnic." I filled everyone in on the details of our brief, but very effective, negotiation with Mr. Frumpy Crab.

"Of course, it's not like we have a written contract or a treaty or whatever, but I think they'll keep their end of the bargain."

"They were scared right out of their carapaces when this high muckety-muck's personal bodyguard turned into six Sploig right in front of them." Kely grinned and nodded to Turk. "Sending over the robosassin flushed them out and when the Sploig shot Harry point-blank and his tux shrugged it off like a spitball, us poor defenseless humans didn't look quite so defenseless."

Gertrude looked a little stunned.

"Uh, let me get this straight: You showed the crabs how they'd been infiltrated by the Sploig, displayed the Sploig superior technology and how we've assimilated it, and blackmailed the crabs into granting Earth sovereignty with promises to help them fight the Sploig?"

"Well, yeah, that, but the whole cheese issue is still up in the air."

"The *cheese* issue?" Gertrude looked worried. "What cheese issue?"

"Well, it turns out they know a lot more about who, where and how we produce cheese than we thought. They're using cheese as a political tool to foster support for the established regime, so, naturally, they want to keep it illegal, illicit and worthy of lots of political support. That'll be hard if Earth is independent. It'd be best for us if it was legal, but that won't work for them."

"So what did you decide?"

"We agreed to make a deal. No details were hammered out, of course, since we were a little pressed for time and the ship was infested with Sploig, but I think it'll turn out to be some kind of partnership to continue the War on Cheese. They'll secretly support cheese production and distribution, and we'll pay them a tidy sum not to bomb the planet to slag." I made a calming motion at everyone's horrified looks. "Don't worry. The bombing is an empty threat and everyone knows it. They'd be killing the golden goose if they really did destroy our cheese-production capacity."

"And what about the Sploig?" Turk asked

"The Sploig are everyone's problem. Now that we know that they know about our cheese production, we're actually on the same side against the Sploig. We keep the technology we've discovered and agree to let the Farfnians know, through the proper channels, of course, whenever there's a Sploig threat."

"And you did all that in thirty minutes in a ship infested with Sploig?" Gertrude gave me her you-gotta-be-kidding-me look and said, "You gotta be kidding me."

"Well, the robosassin made a good bargaining chip, and it didn't hurt to be wearing a tux that can shrug off a round from an ion cannon." I shrugged. "We had all the cards. They just didn't know it, so I had to tell them."

"Well, I'll be a…" Gertrude broke into uncontrollable laughter, which seemed infectious. In short order, even Zook's kids were bubbling over with mirth, though they probably didn't know why. I didn't really get the joke either, but laughing felt good.

"I'm going to go check on Zook. Kik, can you turn us around and get us back to Apollo Station?"

“Can a Carpoolian drool?” She unzipped her jumper and stepped out of it on the way to the pilot’s couch without even breaking stride.

“Right.” I picked my eyeballs up off the deck and put them back in their sockets. “Gertrude, would you see if the *Limburger*’s captain can come to the bridge and maybe do something besides cower?”

“Sure, Harry,” she said as I exited the bridge. To my surprise, three of Zook’s kids followed me out. It felt a little strange to be escorted by a copy of myself, one of Kik and one of Mishi, but they seemed harmless enough.

I really should know better than to think things like that.

CHAPTER ELEVEN

IMMORTAL EDUCATION

Okay, changing clothes with three Immortals, albeit children, standing and watching every move I made because they refused to wait outside my cabin during the process, was a little unnerving. Especially when they started trying to help. Extra especially when the ship did a double shift out of and into stringspace just when one of them was learning how to use a zipper.

Ouch.

I made it to Medical reasonably unscathed and found Zook lying in a bed swathed in enough Derma-Gen® to make two mummy movies and still have enough left to reupholster your couch. Mishi, apparently the original one, not one of Zook's kids—and there was a little confusion here, because Zook's kids were starting to fib about whether they were really Zook's kids or not—was feeding him soup and talking a blue streak.

"And so one of them goes up and gives Lord Colston a big hug, and wouldn't you know it's a copy of Kik, and his wife turns about the same shade as me!" He laughed and shoveled more soup into Zook's mouth. "She was really hot until your kid turned into a perfect copy of Lord Colston; then she just fainted."

"Hi, I'm Kik!" one of Zook's kids said as she flounced up to me in a poor attempt to copy Kik's distinctive swagger.

"Uh, no, you're not Kik. You're one of Zook's kids, but it's very nice to meet you anyway." I shook her hand as she did a remarkably accurate imitation of Kik's pout.

"So, how are you feeling, Daddy?" I asked Zook, more to change the subject than anything.

"Oh, I'm okay, Harry, but I'm a little sore." He accepted another mouthful of soup and swallowed. "Everyone's been so helpful. Especially Kik and Mishi."

"He's pumped full of more drugs than you'd find at a screech-and-roll concert, Harry, but he'll be fine." Mishi kept shoveling soup, most of it ending up in Zook's mouth. "He's lost a lot of body fluids, and the trauma left him in shock, but he's tougher than he looks."

"Hey! We're both Kik!" one of Zook's kids said to the other copy of my pilot. They laughed at some private Immortal joke and started whispering. Girls…

"So how was giving birth, Zook?" I really should have known better than to ask, but as he'd been looking forward to it so much, not asking would have been rude.

"Painful, Harry. A lot more than I thought it would be." He took another mouthful of soup and swallowed. "All things considered, I think I'll avoid it in the future."

"Yeah, it was pretty ugly when they started poppin' out of him like giant zits exploding," Mishi said with all the tact of a…well…a Turpenoid. "These little jelly kind of things were shooting all over the place, and Kik was the only one who wasn't totally freaking out. Boy, she's got some nerve, I tell ya! Too bad about her dress, though."

"Yes, it was…interesting," Zook added, sounding utterly exhausted, which was understandable.

"Well, your kids are causing quite a stir, Zook," I said just as the two copies of Kik came over to me and started fingering the lapels of my jumper. "They're very…uh… inquisitive."

"Oh, they are insatiably curious for the first few months, Harry." Zook perked up a little, either interested in the subject of his kids' development, or entertained by my discomfort as the two Kiks started fiddling with my hair. "You must understand that they are only trying to blend in. At first this was very disturbing for them, since Kik was the only person available for them to mimic. One of them panicked and mimicked an avocado that was on the tray that Mishi brought, then Charlie came by with a few spare jumpers, and several of them decided to mimic him."

"You should've seen the look on Charlie's face, Harry," Mishi said with an evil little Turpenoid laugh. "Six perfect copies of Kik, all butt-naked and trying to hug him all at once. Then they all fall down and he's looking at six copies of himself. I think he's going to have nightmares."

"I can imagine," I said, disentangling one of the Kik-copy's fingers from my belt buckle.

"They are starving for interaction, Harry. They will learn very quickly, but until they are able to blend in, things will be very strange for them."

"For everyone else, too," Mishi said, shoveling the last of the soup into Zook's mouth, then heading for the door. "I'll be back with something more substantial. Later, Zookie!"

"Goodbye, Mishi, and thank you." Zook looked very tired, and I didn't want to stretch his endurance too far, but there were a few questions I had to ask.

"I'm a little concerned about what might happen with your kids doing their mimic trick, Zook. Did anyone tell the guests that these weren't Sploig?"

"Oh, yes. Don't worry, Harry." Zook smiled at his kids. "They will not hurt anyone. When they have all assumed forms they like, most will disperse, or find other species they wish to mimic."

I keep forgetting that Zook hasn't always been human, and curiosity got the best of me. "What were you before you were human, anyway?"

"I thought you knew." He looked a little uncomfortable. "I was a Farfnian, Harry."

That left me a little stunned, but it kind of made sense. Zook had taught me a lot about the crabs: how they think, how they organize, and how they operate socially. He's one of the reasons I've been so successful at not getting caught over the years.

"So, how are you feeling?" I asked, changing the subject with all the aplomb of a porcupine in a balloon factory.

"To tell you the truth, Harry, I'm feeling rather spent." He made a funny face, one I don't think I'd ever seen him make before. "All things considered, I'm glad I experienced it, but I don't think I'll be doing it again. Sixteen is enough." He looked a little drained.

"We'll get you patched up good as new, Zook. Just sit back, relax and don't worry."

"Oh, I'm not worried, Harry. There's a lot of damage, but one morph will solve that problem."

My jaw dropped, but I caught it and put it back in place.

"Morph? You mean you're going to change?"

"I think it's time, Harry. I don't want my offspring to become dependent on me, and I think I have helped you all that I can."

"You mean you're leaving, too?"

The entire universe seemed to drop out from under me for a moment, but then I realized that the ship had just dropped out of stringspace. We were back in the Sol system and would be landing at Apollo Station in a heartbeat.

I tried to talk Zook out of leaving, but that was like trying to talk someone out of their chosen religious belief. All it did was make my mouth tired.

"I'm not leaving right away, but soon. Besides, Harry, you will have some of me here." He nodded to his offspring. "And it seems that some of them have become quite enamored of you."

This was evidenced by two copies of Kik running their fingers through my hair, which was a little uncomfortable… Well, not exactly uncomfortable as much as embarrassing. Okay, it wouldn't have been embarrassing if it hadn't been so arousing. And it wouldn't have been arousing if they hadn't been perfect copies of Kik. And if they really were *perfect* copies of Kik…

"Uh, Zook, I gotta ask, just how closely do you mimic? I mean, your mind, your personality, is you, and that stays the same, right?"

"For the most part, yes, Harry."

"For the most part?"

"Well, yes. You see, there is some adjustment depending on the genetic makeup of the individual being mimicked. For instance, when I was a Farfnian, I thought like a Farfnian. Then I mimicked a human, and now I think like a human. I imagine those of my offspring who have mimicked Mishi are thinking like Turpenoids."

"Yeah, I understand that part, but what about individual…uh…proclivities? I mean, if you mimicked a sociopath, would you be a sociopath?"

"What is a sociopath?"

"Huh?"

"Oh, I know the literal definition, but in real terms, considering the thousands of societal structures of even your limited species, what *is* a sociopath?" This was very hard to concentrate on with two perfect copies of Kik so close and whispering all kinds of interesting things to one another. I was trying not to listen.

Yeah…

"What I really mean, Zook, is if these two," I indicated the two of his offspring who were currently making me very uncomfortable, "are really perfect copies of Kik, do they have her…uh…unique sense of…uh…things?"

"You mean, are they xenophiles?"

"Uh, yeah…that."

"Well, they very well might be."

"And, since they are really not human, they might, uh…"

"Oh, I see what you mean. Well, they just might. Why don't you ask them?"

"Ask them?"

"Yes, Harry. Ask them if they find you attractive."

"You're kidding."

"Not at all. This would be very educational for them, and probably quite enjoyable for you. Why not?"

"They're just kids, Zook. *Your* kids." I cringed as both Kik-copies laughed that breathy Kik laugh. "It wouldn't be right."

"Why not?"

"Uh…" While not being able to verbalize one specific reason why having sex with two of Zook's barely two-hour-old children would be wrong, the number of reasons that registered in my head were too many to enumerate. "Trust me, Zook. It would be wrong."

"Okay, Harry, but it seems kind of silly to me. They are all very curious for anything they can learn about how to blend in to their chosen forms. Learning about sexual interactions in a bisexual species would be invaluable."

"Invaluable?" I guess everything is valuable from a certain perspective. One man's junk is another man's treasure, right?

"Why, yes, Harry. Blending in is paramount in the psychological makeup of every Immortal. If we stand out, we will be discriminated against for being different."

"So your innate desire is to be as normal as possible?" Knowing Zook, this seemed unlikely.

"Well, some of us have lived long enough to have realized our full potential, and so have chosen to interact with other species openly, without regard for self-preservation."

"But still, they're your kids, Zook. I wouldn't feel right about it." Okay, with two copies of Kik breathing in my ears, that was very hard to say. I might feel very *good* about it, but I probably wouldn't feel *right* about it, if you know what I mean.

"Well, okay, Harry, but I still think it's silly."

The ship jerked slightly, which usually meant we were either landing or being shot at. The intercom confirmed my suspicions when Turk's distinctive baritone blared out with ear-splitting intensity.

"We have landed at Apollo Station. All guests are encouraged to disembark in an orderly fashion through the primary air lock on deck three. Have a nice day."

"I better get back to the bridge. Turk's technically in command, which could be a problem."

"Yes, Harry." Zook looked frightened for the first time since I'd known him, which says something about Turk's capacity for command. "You better get back to the bridge."

I started to leave and the two copies of Kik promptly fell in step beside me. This just wouldn't do. Aside from being way too tempting, it would be bad for ship morale for the crew to see me being escorted in such a manner. All kinds of rumors would start flying around, and some of them would probably end up being true. So, in an attempt to stabilize ship morale—uh-huh—I convinced them to stay with Daddy for a while. He could teach them much more than I could, after all, albeit of a different subject matter.

On the way to the bridge I ran across six more of Zook's kids, all accompanied by members of the crew or passengers, and all getting along very well indeed. A little too well, in fact. So well that I had to break up a clinch between a female cargo handler and one of Zook's kids, and let me tell you, it was a little embarrassing when I found myself looking into my own face.

"Oh, Captain Fische! I'm sorry! I was just, you know, being friendly." She tugged at the grinning Immortal's sleeve and led him away. "They're so *curious*, you know."

Great.

Heading back toward the bridge, a whole new slew of worries about rumors raced through my head. There were copies of me running around being *friendly* with the crew. Who knew what I might end up getting blamed for. Or *sued* for. Or *charged* with and, considering that they mimic the DNA of the people they copy, *convicted* of using genetic evidence. Yes, this could be bad.

I punched the button to summon the lift, trying to think of some way to staunch the flood of potential rumors. The door opened and I almost ran into another copy of my pilot. This was getting ridiculous!

"Oh, sorry. Going up?"

"Down," she answered, smiling and stepping aside.

"I'll just ride along." I stepped in and punched the button for the bridge. If I wasn't so lazy I would have just walked up two flights of steps, but given the option of climbing stairs or sharing an elevator with a beautiful woman, I will always take the latter, even if she is only a copy, and two hours old, and incredibly sexy, and looking at me as if she'd like to learn all the wonders of the human species.

The lift doors closed and we started down. It was only one floor, but it seemed like a long time. She was looking at me, and I was trying not to look at her and failing horribly. I kept asking myself silly questions like "Who would know?" and "Why not?"

The lift stopped and the doors opened, but the copy of Kik didn't get out. She shuffled from foot to foot a little, then looked up at me with eyes that were just way too big and way too blue and asked, "Are you ever curious about…things?"

"Uh, yeah. Yeah, I'm curious about a *lot* of things." Okay, so I was babbling. No excuses. My mouth just says stuff sometimes when my brain's not listening. Maybe it's a software glitch.

“Me, too,” she said, smiling that smile that turned the knob on her “hottie-o-meter” way past the maximum that is humanly possible.

“Nothing wrong with being curious.” Yeah, that’s right. I was just curious.

“Nothing at all.” She reached out and touched my hand.

This is bad, my conscience said in my ear. *This is not right. This is Zook’s child.*

“Would you like to…uh…,” my mouth said, ignoring my foolish conscience, as usual.

“Follow me,” she said, pulling me out of the lift just as the doors closed.

I could have stopped it. I could have pulled away and listened to my conscience. Okay, maybe I couldn’t have, because when you’re being led by the hand by a beautiful woman and both of you have the same thing on your mind, there is a force of nature that simply turns off all reasoning portions of the human mind, be it synthetic or organic, and you revert to the happy, happy monkey that dwells deep down inside all of us.

And happy, happy monkeys don’t think.

I didn’t think. I didn’t know where we were going and I didn’t care when we got there. There was too much to experience, too much to touch and feel and taste. The reasoning portion of my mind simply took a vacation.

I was very, *very* happy.

CHAPTER TWELVE

THE JIG IS UP

When the reasoning portion of my mind finally beat a hole through the haze of afterglow, the image of my surroundings coalesced into my consciousness and I came to a sudden and shocking realization.

"These are Kik's quarters."

"Of course they're my quarters. Where else would I take you?"

The voice, the intonation, the surroundings; things were adding up to a very uncomfortable sum in my head. I rolled over and looked into her eyes, just as she came to the same sum from a different equation.

"But how did you know these were my quarters if you're…"

We stared at each other, our faces no more than a few inches apart, and realized what we had just done.

"Uh-oh."

"Harry?"

"Yeah," I said, almost apologetically. "Kik?"

"Uh-huh."

"I thought you were—"

"I thought you were, too!"

We both jumped out of her bed and started reaching for clothes, one of the most uncomfortable moments of my life, I might add. After a moment of confusion and a quick trade of garments, we started babbling and reaching for shoes and socks.

"I'm sorry, Kik. I really did think you were one of Zook's kids. I don't know what came over me."

"I'm sorry, too! I thought you were an Immortal! Honest! I've never…I mean, this is the first time I ever…you know…with a *human*!" Her voice climbed to a hysterical pitch. She looked at me in horror, clutching the front of her jumper with white-knuckled fury. "I've never been with a *man* before!"

"Well, think of me as a cyborg, if that helps." I was almost sure it wouldn't help, but I was a little short on constructive suggestions.

"But…but…but…"

It is always a bad sign when women do this. It means their reasoning ability has flown the coop and they are functioning completely on emotion. Lots of emotion. Tears usually follow, then throwing things, and lots of yelling. I didn't know if I could handle that right now, so I figured a different tack might work. I mean, after all, this was Kik, right?

"Was I that bad?"

"Huh?"

Well, at least I stopped the "but…but's."

"Was the last thirty minutes…" I checked my watch, which happened to be hanging from a light fixture. "Okay, was the last *forty* minutes really that unpleasant?"

"Well, no." That was a bonus

"It seemed to me you rather enjoyed it."

"Well, yeah." Another bonus. "But that doesn't mean I'm…I'm…"

"It doesn't *mean* anything, Kik." I dropped my boot and rounded the foot of the bed, a bed we had just put through enough product testing to earn a Romp-O-Rama® seal of approval, mind you. "It means we both thought we were someone else and that we both had a very pleasant encounter."

"Pleasant?" A little steel crept back into her voice, which was exactly what I was hoping for. "I was just *pleasant*?"

"Very pleasant," I amended, not knowing if I should go so far as to unload the entire truth right here and now.

"Pleasant is candy and flowers, Harry. I think it was more than pleasant."

"Okay, it was wonderful," I admitted, still not sure if she was fully back to herself.

"*Wonderful* sounds like a nice dinner, maybe some dancing—which you still owe me, by the way—but not what just happened here, Harry."

“Okay, what would you call it?”

“I would say that if the moon was tectonically active, we would have rearranged a few plates! Heaven and Hell could have fought the last battle in this room and neither of us would have noticed! Admit it!”

“Uh…well, okay. Yeah. That.” Now I was a little dumbfounded. Had it been *that* good? I played a few memories back in my head. “Wow. I never…” I played a few more, and my knees started shaking. “I mean, I thought it would be…but…wow.”

“Yeah. That.” She sat down, and I noticed her knees were shaking, too. “So, what do we *do* about it, Harry?”

“Do?” I asked, all the myriad possibilities of what that word could mean rambling through my head like a stampede of wild armadillos. “Define ‘do’.”

“That’s what I mean, Harry.” She stood and started pacing, which was a little dangerous in a twelve-by-twelve-foot stateroom. “I mean, I’m not ready to change my lifestyle just because we had the most amazing sex I’ve ever experienced, and I don’t think you would want to have me hanging around thinking I was missing out on something every time a species I haven’t been with happens by, so how do we come to grips with what we just experienced and what we know we can’t have, and what we want, but might not *really* want when we think about what we had before, and then—”

“Kik! Stop!”

“Huh?”

“We don’t have to *do* anything.”

“But…but…but…”

We were back in panic mode and there was only one way I could think of that would break the downward spiral.

“Kik! Wait! Listen to me.”

“Uh, okay.”

“You don’t owe me anything and I don’t owe you anything. We both had the time of our lives, with each other, and that is something we will always have. I don’t expect anything else from you but that memory.” A memory I could play back like a video any time I wanted, by the way. In fact, I’m playing it back right now. Woo hoo!

"But everyone else will think—"

"Nobody else has to *know*, Kik." That brought her up short. "With all the copies of you and me running around this ship, we could have both been Zook's kids for all anyone knows."

"You mean we could *lie*?" A glimmer of hope shone in her eyes, and I felt a twinge of regret for the suggestion.

"Well, to everyone else, sure. We would always know, of course, but it's something we could just share." Her brows knitted, and I realized what that sounded like, so I added, "No obligations. No debts. No expectations. We can just share the memory and leave it at that."

"You'd be satisfied with that?"

I thought I heard a little remorse in her tone, which plucked my heartstrings like a harp with only one string left. After all the years I'd longed for this to happen, I now had to convince Kik that I'd be okay with "just being friends."

Uh, yeah… I could do that.

"I could be, if you want me to be." Not very convincing, I'll admit, but my heart wasn't in it. No way I'd be satisfied with anything less than taking her by hand and never letting go every again, but saying I could be brought a smile to her lips, which made it worth it. Kind of.

"And nobody would have to know?"

"Not if you don't want them to."

"Well, okay. I just need some time to think about this. I mean, it's hard for me to get my head around, if you know what I mean." She stood there kneading her hands and biting her lip.

"Kik, I've been seduced by a Sploig. I know *exactly* what you mean."

"Oh, sure, bring *that* up!"

"Huh?"

"Oh, come on, Harry. You *know* I'm jealous about that. I was dying to have a little one-on-one time with a Sploig."

"Well, first of all, I didn't even know they were Sploig when we…uh…were together, and second, it was more like one on four." I did a little shiver with the memory of Laila forming up from four bits of silvery protoplasm. "And it wasn't all that, anyway."

“Wasn’t all what?” she asked as I recovered my boots.

“All that,” I said, nodding to her disheveled bed. “Not even close.”

“Well, maybe I didn’t miss much after all.” She slipped on her shoes and moved to the door. “I’ll just go see how Zook’s doing. You better get to the bridge. Turk was looking like he wanted to shoot something, and Ernie showed up and was trying to tell everyone what to do.”

“Oh, crap. I shouldn’t have asked Gertrude to see if he wanted to help.”

She keyed the door open, we stepped out into the corridor…and stopped.

“Well, it’s about damn time you two hooked up.” Gertrude took her hands off her more-than-ample hips and clapped them together. “Now can we get this bucket of bolts back to Earth? I’ve got a lot of work to do with all the mess you made.”

I glanced up and down the corridor, but Gertrude was the only one in sight.

“If we kill her, nobody will know,” I said to Kik in a conspiratorial whisper intentionally loud enough for Gertrude to hear. I was slightly gratified that my assistant’s eyes widened for a moment before narrowing with her usual skepticism.

“We’d have to hide the body,” Kik whispered back, and I was pleased at the lack of panic in her voice. Maybe she was serious. “And I don’t know anyplace on the ship big enough to—”

“Oh, now you better just stop right there, Kikira, unless you want to find your skinny white ass kicked right up between your skinny white shoulder blades.” She did one of those full-body shimmies that prize fighters do right before they start swinging, so I thought I’d step in.

“Kik, why don’t you go check on Zook and let me have a little talk with Gertrude.”

“But, Harry, I—”

“Trust me on this, Kik.” I turned and gave her a little smile that I hoped instilled confidence.

“Fine.” Okay, there was more worry than confidence there, but at least we weren’t reverting to panic. “I’ll see you on the bridge.” She shot a glare at Gertrude and walked away.

"Now, Gertrude," I started, but I stopped at her upraised hands and the look she was giving me.

"I don't want to know and I don't really care, Harry. We've got too much to do for me to worry about your sex life."

"My sex life, or lack thereof, is *nobody's* business, Gertrude." I tried to put a little steel in my tone, but I probably only managed aluminum. "And what's your hurry?"

"We've got to get back to Earth to clean up this mess before the (expletive deleted) hits the air conditioning."

"Mess? What mess?" That was the second time she referred to our situation as a mess, and I was a little bothered by the reference. "I thought I'd just cleaned up a mess."

"Oh? Well, I think you just opened a whole pile of new ones!"

"What do you mean? I just negotiated an independent planetary charter for Earth! You know what that means? We get to govern ourselves again. No more Farfnian interference!"

"Oh? And you think Earth Gov is ready for that?" Her hands were back on her hips, and she was talking in that I-must-be-speaking-to-an-idiot tone that I hated so much. "You think they'll do *one* thing right? You think they know jack (expletive deleted) about what's really goin' on in the galaxy?"

"Well, no, but—"

"Damn right they don't!" She grabbed my wrist and started dragging me toward the bridge. "And we've got to make damn sure they learn before the whole thing blows up in their faces."

"Oh? And how are *we* going to do that?"

That was when she stopped, looked me squarely in the eye and said, "We aren't. *You* are," and continued dragging me toward the bridge, not explaining a thing.

So, here I sit, telling you, a perfect stranger, all of my worries while I wait for Gertrude to come fetch me out of this dive and explain what the hell she meant about me teaching Earth Gov what's really going on in the galaxy.

Not that they'd believe me, even if I told them the truth.

(excerpt deleted)

Huh? Hey, wait a second. Who are you guys?

(sounds of scuffle)

Hey! Ouch! Hey, wait!

Record # KR29387/y. Transcript ends.

All of my interrogators look at me as the recording ends.

The silence is deafening.

I try to get comfortable in the hard plastic chair, but I've been sitting in it for twelve hours and there are too many eyes on me for comfort to be an achievable goal, even if I'd been sitting in my Corinthian leather superchair. Even if my wrists weren't handcuffed behind my back.

"The sound quality sucks," I say, trying for nonchalant. I don't feel very nonchalant, of course, but I'm not about to let them know that.

Things aren't looking too good. The evidence is overwhelming. Even if the audio quality sucks, it's enough to lock me away forever and then some.

"These recordings took more than a year to procure, Harold Fische," one of my interrogators says, ejecting the tiny disc from the player and holding it up before my eyes with one hand and patting the three thick transcripts with the other. "They're the result of thousands of hours of meticulous surveillance and great personal risk by our deep-cover operatives."

"It's the result of my big mouth and too much scotch," I counter, disgusted with myself for falling for such a bonehead ploy. I've always talked too much when I've had a few drinks, cyber-brain or no cyber-brain. "And the only thing your operatives might have risked was a nasty hangover."

"Irregardless," another of my interrogators interjects, "we have enough evidence to convict you on dozens of charges and to discern the location of your illegal narcotics factory—"

"It's a dairy," I counter, "and *irregardless* isn't a word."

"Animals of the family Bovidae are illegal on this planet, Mister Fische. You have been engaging in illegal activities, producing a narcotic substance from the lactational secretions of these animals, and selling it on the black market!"

"Speak human," I said, giving him The Look. I've had just about enough of this. They would either charge me, try me, and lock me up, or deal. "I've been making and selling cheese to

Farfnians. I made more money doing so in the last two months than Earth's entire *legal* GPP for the last ten years. Most of that money was pumped right back into *your* economy. You tell me what *Earth* law I broke."

"Earth Government's constitution clearly states—"

"Earth Gov's constitution was written by Farfnians!" I've got virtually nothing to lose here, so playing the heavy is a no-brainer. "If you wanted to charge me, you would have charged me already. Shit or get off the pot, boys. I'm here because you need me, not because you like my sense of humor."

I sit back and consider whether or not I have gone over the line. I don't think I have, but I could be wrong. It wouldn't be the first time. I've always had trouble with lines.

My interrogators remain silent for a bit, apparently taken aback by my little tirade. These are people who are used to being taken seriously, who are used to being feared. I'm either too powerful or too stupid to fear them or take them seriously; it's fun sitting here watching them try to figure out which.

The door opens and a middle-aged human walks in. I recognize her immediately; she's the president of Earth Gov. Everyone in the room comes to attention, and despite myself, I sit up in my uncomfortable plastic chair.

"Mister Fische, you must realize that you are in an untenable position," she says, exuding all the power her position allows—which really isn't much, by my standards.

"I've been in a lot of positions, Ms. President," I say, wondering if she'll get my double entendre. Nope, not even an eyebrow twitch. Figures. "Some have been less tenable than others, yet here I sit, alive, whole for the most part, and trying to figure out exactly what you want from me."

"We want you to be *honest* with us, Mister Fische." There is emotion in her voice now and though she is a consummate politician and can dial emotions like I dial for pizza, I think this one's real. "We need to know what you know. We need to be able to deal with the Farfnians on their own terms if we are to salvage anything at all from this debacle."

"Debacle?" I'm taken aback. "I hand you an independent planetary charter on a silver plate and you call it a debacle?"

“Yes, well, Mister Fische, there is the premise that one must *do* something with such a charter. And, you see, we don’t really know what, essentially, *to* do.”

I examine my captors while trying to keep my jaw from dropping. I realize, finally, that not a single one of them has probably ever been out of the solar system, or spoken directly with any extraterrestrial other than a Farfnian stooge. I try to formulate something intelligent to say, something helpful, but I can’t. I can only think of one thing.

“You all need to get out more.”

“Now, see here, Mister Fische! You are under arrest for trafficking in—”

“That’s *enough*, Clarence!” The president’s voice is laced with all the power she can muster, which, being president of a backwater dirtball, isn’t much, but it’s enough to cow these sheep…er…yeah.

“Mister Fische, you are here for two reasons: first and foremost, you may be able to help us in dealing with extraterrestrial species, given your experience in…uh…the galactic marketplace. Second, you were foolish enough to allow us to capture you.”

“I wasn’t foolish. I was careless. There’s a difference.” Well, not really, but I want to know if they know that.

“Carelessness is foolish *by* definition, Mister Fische. You are not as smart as you think. You were foolish enough that we were able to trap you, even with our admittedly limited resources.” She stands there smugly, totally missing her own point. It’s time to teach her a little humility.

“You trapped me because you understand humans. That ought to tell you something about the crabs. If it doesn’t, you’re dimmer than I thought and I really can’t help you.”

“You understand them better than they understand us. That’s simple.”

“I’m impressed,” I say, not really impressed but willing to concede that she has a vague grasp of the situation. “Now, why am I here again?”

“Because we need your expertise with extraterrestrials. I thought I made that clear.”

"No, that's why you *think* I'm here, but it's not *really* why I'm here." I love this part, and I can't help but smile.

"Am I *missing* something, Mister Fische?"

"Oh, see, now I've gone and made you mad. I'm sorry." Not really. Not even a little. In fact, I was trying to accomplish just that, just to make a point. "You see, expertise is nothing without resources."

"Resources?"

They are all still completely in the dark. No wonder the Farfnians walk all over them.

"Yes, resources." I shift my position slightly, trying to ease the discomfort in my shoulders and butt. "As you may have noticed, Earth is a little short on resources when it comes to anything of value on the galactic market."

"Except for cheese," she says, enlightenment finally dawning on her plain political features.

"Except for cheese," I agree, shifting again and wincing in pain. "Now, you don't really *have* any cheese, do you?"

Some uncomfortable glances shoot around the room; none, I notice, from my immediate adversary, the president. She's finally catching on.

"But cheese is illegal, and will remain illegal under the agreement I made with the Farfnians," I add, cocking an eyebrow at her. "And Earth Gov can't deal with something illegal. But what you don't know is that we have more than just cheese to bargain with."

"This technology you say you possess. Alien technology." Her tongue darts out to wet her lips.

There it is. That's what she's really after.

"If Earth possessed that technology, we would be a force to be reckoned with." She says that slowly, almost smiling.

"No."

"No?"

"No, we wouldn't be a force to be reckoned with, because if the crabs get the barest whiff that Earth is using alien technology to beef up its military, this planet will be a smoldering ruin before you can say 'Holy shit, would you look at that asteroid!'"

Okay, even under duress, my eloquence is all it has ever been.

"Then what other resource do we possess that can be used as a bargaining tool with the Farfnians, Mister Fische?"

She's really torqued now, which is right where I want her. People, human or alien, don't think as clearly when they are angry. That is my secret, my ace in the hole; I'm really, really good at pissing people off, and when their dander is up and their pants are down, I strike.

"*Information*, Ms. President." I wince again at the ache in my handcuffed arms. "If I were made a little more comfortable, I might be inclined to share some of that information."

"Oh, you think *this* is discomfort, Mister Fische?" Her voice takes on a dark tone that I do not like at all. "You don't know what discomfort is until you've walked a mile in *my* shoes."

I look down at her sensible pumps and grimace. "I'm really not into cross-dressing, but if you insist, I wear an eleven triple-E."

"Your weak attempts at sarcastic humor do not impress me, Mister Fische, and you are *not* getting out of this without putting something on the table."

I give her my best disinterested scoff and say, "Is this where you tell me I play ball or spend the rest of my life in a very unpleasant little cell with a large fellow by the name of Bruno?"

"No, Mister Fische, this is where I tell you that you are about to become the most powerful human in the galaxy, like it or not."

Now *that* catches me off guard.

"Huh?"

She doesn't respond to my razor-sharp retort, but turns and starts for the door.

"What are you talking about? You're going to coerce me by threatening to make me your ambassador or something?"

She turns back and gives me a feral smile. "No, Mister Fische, I'm going to coerce you by making you President of Earth Gov."

As my jaw falls into my lap, she directs her wrath to her cronies.

"Elect him."

"Elect *me*? What do you mean, elect me? I'm not running for office!" My pleas go unheeded as she opens the door and slams it closed behind her. *President of Earth Gov?* "I don't even *like* politics!"

I know she can still hear me, so I scream out one last defiant appeal. "I'm not even a registered voter!"

We hope you have enjoyed the Cheese Runner's Trilogy

Cheese Runners
Cheese Rustlers
Cheese Lords

Available in audio, electronic, and print formats

About the Author

From the sea to the stars, Chris A. Jackson's stories take you to the far reaches of the imagination. Raised on the back deck of a fishing boat and trained as a marine biologist, he became sidetracked by a career in biomedical research, but regained his heart and soul in 2009 when he and his wife Anne left the dock aboard the 45-foot sailboat *Mr Mac* to cruise the Caribbean and write fulltime.

With his nautical background, writing sea stories seemed inevitable for Chris. His acclaimed Scimitar Seas nautical fantasies won three consecutive Gold Medals in the *ForeWord Reviews* Book of the Year Awards. His Pathfinders Tales from Paizo Publishing combine high-seas combat and romance set in the award-winning world of the Pathfinder Roleplaying Game. Not to be outdone, Privateer Press released *Blood & Iron*, a swashbuckling novella set in the Iron Kingdoms.

Chris' repertoire also includes the award-winning and Kindle best-selling Weapon of Flesh Series, the contemporary urban fantasy *Dragon Dreams*, as well as additional fantasy novels, the humorous sci fi Cheese Runners trilogy of novellas, and numerous short stories.

To learn more, please visit jaxbooks.com.

Novels by Chris A. Jackson

From Jaxbooks
A Soul for Tsing
Deathmask

Weapon of Flesh Trilogy
Weapon of Flesh
Weapon of Blood
Weapon of Vengeance

Weapon of Flesh Trilogy II
(with Anne L. McMillen-Jackson)
Weapon of Fear
Weapon of Pain
Weapon of Mercy (summer 2017)

The Cornerstones Trilogy
(with Anne L. McMillen-Jackson)
Zellohar
Nekdukarr
Jundag

The Cheese Runners Trilogy
(novellas)
Cheese Runners
Cheese Rustlers
Cheese Lords

From Dragon Moon Press
Scimitar Moon
Scimitar Sun
Scimitar's Heir
Scimitar War

From Paizo Publishing
Pirate's Honor
Pirate's Promise
Pirate's Prophecy
Pirate's Curse (early 2017)

From Privateer Press
Blood & Iron (ebook novella)

From The Ed Greenwood Group
Hellmaw: Dragon Dreams

Check out these and more at
jaxbooks.com

Want to get an email about my next book release?
Sign up at http://eepurl.com/xnrUL

www.ingramcontent.com/pod-product-compliance
Lightning Source LLC
Chambersburg PA
CBHW070458130626
46555CB00003B/1056
9781939837141